"Everyone who works [...] or another.

"You're no different, Sie[...]

"Yes," she assured him with a smile. "I really am. You came to me, Adam. You needed my help."

A muscle in his jaw twitched and his dark eyes suddenly went even darker. She almost felt some sympathy for him because clearly he didn't like being reminded that he'd had a problem he couldn't solve himself.

"I'm here now and I'll do what we agreed on," she continued. "But don't think you can pull the King of the Universe thing with me."

In an instant the darkness in his eyes lifted and his mouth curved slightly. She really hated what that simple facial expression did to the pit of her stomach. "King of the Universe," he mused. "I like it."

Laughing, she said, "Of course you do." As her laughter faded, her smile remained because the tension had been broken and because damn it, she liked him. Bossy attitude or not.

* * *

Billionaire's Bargain is part of
Harlequin Desire's #1 bestselling series,
Billionaires and Babies: Powerful men...wrapped
around their babies' little fingers.

Dear Reader,

I love writing a Billionaires and Babies book. It's the whole thing of seeing a man who is *not* prepared to be responsible for a baby having to change his opinions fast.

In this book, you'll meet Adam Quinn and Sienna West. Sienna divorced Adam's brother Devon a few years ago but now Adam needs her help. After Devon's death, Adam finds out that he has a six-month-old nephew he never knew about. And the only one he trusts to help him with this situation is Sienna.

Sienna has plenty of reasons to distrust the Quinn family, but her soft heart demands that she help Adam with the baby—at least until he can find the right nanny.

But soon, the two of them discover that there's much more between them than old memories and a child who needs them both.

I really hope you'll enjoy this book because Adam and Sienna are two of my all-time favorite characters. Please visit me on Facebook and let me know what you think of it. I'm always delighted to hear from readers!

Until then, happy reading!

Maureen Child

MAUREEN CHILD

BILLIONAIRE'S BARGAIN

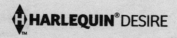

Recycling programs
for this product may
not exist in your area.

ISBN-13: 978-1-335-97153-1

Billionaire's Bargain

Copyright © 2018 by Maureen Child

Printed in U.S.A.

www.Harlequin.com

Maureen Child writes for the Harlequin Desire line and can't imagine a better job. A seven-time finalist for a prestigious Romance Writers of America RITA® Award, Maureen is an author of more than one hundred romance novels. Her books regularly appear on bestseller lists and have won several awards, including a Prism Award, a National Readers' Choice Award, a Colorado Romance Writers Award of Excellence and a Golden Quill Award. She is a native Californian but has recently moved to the mountains of Utah.

Books by Maureen Child

Harlequin Desire

The Baby Inheritance
Maid Under the Mistletoe
The Tycoon's Secret Child
A Texas-Sized Secret
Little Secrets: His Unexpected Heir
Rich Rancher's Redemption
Billionaire's Bargain

Pregnant by the Boss

Having Her Boss's Baby
A Baby for the Boss
Snowbound with the Boss

Visit her Author Profile page at Harlequin.com, or maureenchild.com, for more titles.

To the Canterbury girls—Teresa, Patti, Mary, Colleen and Peggy. For the memories, for the laughs and because I love you guys.

One

"Fifty thousand dollars and the baby's all yours."

Adam Quinn swallowed back a quick jolt of anger and studied his adversary. Kim Tressler was about thirty, with white-blond hair cut into a sharp wedge that clung to her cheeks. She wore a black, body-hugging dress that left little to the imagination. Her heavily lined blue eyes were narrowed on him and her mouth was a grim, red slash. She stood hipshot, with her infant son propped on her left hip.

Deliberately, he kept himself from looking too closely at the baby. His dead brother's son. Adam had to keep his head on straight to deal with this woman and that wouldn't happen if he looked at Devon's child.

Adam was used to handling all sorts of adversaries. Owning one of the world's largest construction and property development companies ensured that Adam regularly went head-to-head with many different types of personalities. And he always found a way to win. This time, though, it wasn't business. It was personal. And it cut damn deep.

Glancing down at the DNA test lying open on his desk, Adam saw proof that the baby's father was Devon Quinn, Adam's younger brother. He kept his gaze fixed on the paperwork even as he admitted silently that the test hadn't been necessary. The baby boy looked just like Devon. So that meant there was no way Adam could leave the baby with his mother. Hell, he wouldn't want to leave a dog with her. Kim came across as cold and mercenary. Exactly the kind of woman Devon would go for. Adam's brother had always had miserable taste in women.

With one major exception. Devon's ex-wife, Sienna West.

Adam felt a flicker of something he didn't want to acknowledge, then deliberately pushed all thoughts of Sienna from his mind. He was dealing with a very different kind of woman at the moment, and he needed to focus.

"Fifty thousand," he repeated, slowly lifting his gaze to hers.

"It's fair." She lifted one shoulder in a careless shrug and when the baby started fussing, she jiggled him furiously to try to silence him. Rather than looking at her child, she slid a fast, careful glance around Adam's office and he knew what she was seeing.

His inner office was huge, with a massive, mahogany desk that now stood between him and the woman. Wide windows offered a spectacular view of the Pacific, where surfers and boaters plied the water's surface. Framed photos of some of his company's more famous projects lined the battleship-gray walls, and wood floors were softened by deep, ruby-colored rugs. He'd worked hard to put his company where it was at the moment and damned if he cared for having her look around like everything in the place had dollar signs on it.

When the infant subsided into whimpers, she shifted her attention back to Adam and said, "Look. This is Devon's child. He promised to take care of me and the baby. He's the one who wanted a kid. Now that he's dead, all of that's over. My career's taking off and I don't have the time to take care of it. I don't want the baby. But since he's Devon's, I'm guessing you do."

No more motherly instinct than a feral cat. In fact, less, he told himself, immediately feeling sorry for the baby. At the same time, Adam couldn't help wondering what the hell his brother had seen in this woman. Even considering that Devon had always been as deep as a puddle, why would he choose to make a child with a woman who was so clearly mercenary? She didn't give a flying damn about her own child—or Adam's brother.

He swallowed hard at how easily she dismissed Devon and his memory. Adam's younger brother had had his issues, but damn it, he deserved better than he was getting from his former lover. But that was Devon. He'd never thought beyond the next adventure. The next woman. Sadly, he'd never had a chance to move on from this one. And though he'd known about his child, he hadn't left a will because he'd expected to live forever.

Instead, he'd died in a horrific boating accident in the south of France just a little over six months ago. That wound was still fresh enough to bring a wave of pain that washed over Adam. When Devon died, it had been a year since Adam had spoken to him. Now he never would.

"Does he have a *name*?" Since she'd only referred to the child as "the baby," Adam wouldn't have been surprised to find she hadn't bothered to name him, either.

"Of course he has a name. It's Jack."

After their father. Adam didn't know whether to be moved or angry. Devon had cut himself off from the family, and then named the child he'd never know after a grandfather dead long before his birth.

Time for introspection later, he warned himself.

"What took you so long to bring the baby to me?"

Adam leaned back in his chair and studied her, still keeping his gaze from straying to the child.

"I've been busy." She shook her hair back from her face and winced when the child slapped one hand against her cheek. "Since all of the publicity revolving around Devon's death, I've had several modeling gigs in France."

Money made on the broken bones of his dead brother. Kim was trading on being Devon's last lover and clearly her child was slowing her down. Fury, ripe and rich, boiled and bubbled in the pit of his stomach and he knew he couldn't afford to let her see it. Damned if Adam wanted to give the bitch a dime, but he also couldn't see himself leaving a defenseless kid with such a cold woman.

She sighed and tapped the toe of her high-heeled sandal against the hardwood floor. "Are you going to pay me or do I—"

"What?" He stood abruptly, planted both hands on his desk and stared into her eyes. He was willing to call her bluff. Remind her that *he* was the one in charge here. She'd come to him, not the other way around. He had the power in this little scuffle and they both knew it. "What exactly will you do, Ms. Tressler? Drop him off at an orphanage? Try to sell him to someone else?"

Sparks fired in her eyes, but wisely, she kept silent.

"We both know you're not going to do either of those things. Mainly, because I'd put my lawyers on you and they'd tangle your career up so tightly you'd be lucky to get a job posing beside a bag of dog food."

Her eyes narrowed and she breathed in fast, shallow gasps.

"You want money, you'll get it." He'd avoided looking at the baby, but he couldn't stand the thought of her even touching Devon's kid a moment longer. He came around the edge of his desk, scooped the baby boy out of her grip and held him uneasily. The child stared at him through wide, unblinking eyes, almost as if he were trying to decide what he thought about the whole thing.

Adam couldn't blame him. The boy had been dragged halfway across the globe, and then handed off to a stranger. It was a wonder he wasn't howling. Hell, it was a wonder *Adam* wasn't howling. He hadn't been around kids much and babies, almost never. By design.

That was, apparently, going to change. Fast.

"Fine. Then let's finish our business and I'll be on my way."

He dismissed her with a cool look, then hit the intercom button on his desk phone. When it took a few seconds for his assistant to answer, he knew Kevin had probably been listening at the door. No doubt, the man was ready to toss Kim Tressler out on her well-toned ass.

"Kevin," he said curtly. "Get legal in here. I need them to draw up an agreement. Now."

"On it."

"Legal?" Kim's eyebrows lifted into high arches.

"You think I'm handing you fifty thousand dollars without making sure it's the *last* time you come to me for money?"

Adam knew her type. Hell, before Devon died, Adam and the company had paid off dozens of women he'd grown tired of. Again, with the exception being Sienna West. When she and Devon had divorced, Sienna had refused a settlement—in spite of the fact that Adam had done everything he could to change her mind.

"What if I don't sign?" Kim asked.

"Oh, you'll sign," Adam told her. "You want the money too much to refuse. And, I'll warn you now, if you try anything—like renegotiating—I'll file for custody. I'll win. I can afford to fight you for years. Hell, by the time everything's settled, you'll be bleaching gray roots. Understood?"

Her mouth worked as if words were gathering there, trying to spill free, but she was holding them back. Finally, she managed to say, "Understood."

There was no way she'd fight him on this. Mainly because she just didn't care enough.

Adam looked at the baby boy in his arms and wondered what the hell he was supposed to do now. Adam knew nothing about babies. There was no family for him to call on for help. His dad was gone and his mother was living in Florida with her latest boyfriend—and she wasn't exactly a "typical" grandma, anyway.

He was going to have to hire someone. A nanny. But until then... Reaching for the intercom button again, he pressed it and said, "Kevin, come in here, will you?"

A second or two later, the office door opened to reveal Kevin Jameson. Tall, with dark blond hair and sharp eyes the same shade of blue as his silk tie, Kevin paused long enough to give the woman in the room a hard look, then walked to Adam. "What do you need?"

Instantly, Adam handed the baby over and just managed to swallow a sigh of relief before it could escape. If the situation had been different, he might have laughed at the expression of pure panic on Kevin's face, but Adam had a feeling his own features hadn't looked much different a minute or two ago. "Take care of him while Kim and I get this situation resolved."

"Me?" Kevin held the baby as he would have a stick of dynamite with a burning fuse.

"Yeah. His stuff is in that bag," Adam added, then waved to the two men in staid black suits entering the room. "Thanks, Kev."

As the lawyers huddled around the desk, Adam didn't watch Kevin and the baby leave. But he knew he'd hear about it later. Kevin and he had been roommates in college, so they went far enough back that he'd feel free to let Adam know just what he thought about being made an instant babysitter.

With the doors closed, Adam looked at Kim and said, "This is it. A onetime payment and you'll sign away all parental rights. Are we clear?"

She didn't look happy—probably because she'd imagined coming back for more money whenever she felt like it. Adam wasn't stupid enough to allow room for that.

"Fine."

Nodding, Adam said, "Gentlemen, write it up. I want a document that turns over care of Devon's infant son to me. And I want one that will stand up in *any* court."

Kim's eyes narrowed. "Seriously? You don't trust me to keep my word?"

"You're selling your son," Adam reminded her tightly. "Why in the hell would I trust you?"

An hour later, Kim Tressler was gone and Kevin was back in Adam's office, his feet propped on the edge of the desk. "I'll get you for handing that baby off to me."

"I figured you would," Adam said, lifting his own feet to the desk. He leaned back in his chair, took a sip of coffee and wished to hell it was scotch. "You heard all of it, right? I mean before you came in to get the kid."

"Damn right I did." Kevin drank his own coffee.

"As soon as I saw her come in with that baby, I knew there was going to be trouble." He shook his head. "Kid looks just like his father. Adam, we both know Devon picked some crappy women in his time, but that one I think takes the prize."

"If they gave prizes for selling your own kid, yeah, she would."

"Man, it's days like these that make me glad I'm gay."

Adam snorted, then stopped. Looked around. "Where's the baby?"

Kevin laid his head back and closed his eyes. "I put Kara in charge of him. She's got three kids of her own, so I figured, hey. Experience counts."

"Plus, then you didn't have to watch him."

"Major bonus, yes." Kevin opened one eye to look at Adam. "I noticed you weren't real anxious to cuddle up, either."

"Well what the hell do I know about babies?"

"And you think I magically know something?" Kevin shuddered. "Kara's taking care of him and I sent Teddy from accounting out to buy diapers and food and whatever the hell else it needs."

"He. Not it."

"Excuse me."

"Okay, so the baby's fine for now. But that won't last." Adam frowned. He needed help and he needed it now. "I have to find a nanny."

"Well don't look at me."

"I wouldn't do that to the kid."

"Funny." Kevin took another sip of coffee and sighed. "So do you want me to set up interviews or something?"

He could trust Kevin not only to advertise, but to interview and find the best possible person for any given job. Still, this was something he should probably do himself. "I'll take care of it. But I need someone *today*."

"Yeah, that's not gonna happen."

"What about your mom?" Adam asked, delighted when that brilliant idea popped into his mind. Kevin's mother had practically adopted Adam into the family years ago. She was warm, kind, funny and already a grandmother thanks to Kevin's sister Nora. "You think she'd help me out for a while?"

"She'd love it," Kevin said, nodding. "Nothing Anna Jameson likes better than a baby."

"Good—"

"Unfortunately for you," Kevin added, "she's on that Alaskan cruise you gave her for her birthday…"

"Damn it." Scowling, Adam took another drink of his coffee.

"Got a video email from her last night," Kevin said. "She and Aunt Noreen are having a great time. Mom bought Nick and I fur coats for winter."

"We live in Southern California."

Kevin shrugged. "Didn't seem to matter to Mom. Oh, and she said to say thank you again."

"She's welcome again. Your sister lives in San Diego, so I can't ask her."

"Nora's got three of her own. If you don't mind the drive she probably wouldn't even notice a fourth."

"Funny. I just wish—never mind." Adam looked at his friend. "Who else do we know?"

"Any number of people." Kevin shrugged. "None of whom I'd trust with a baby. Except for maybe Nick—and before you suggest it, no."

Kevin's husband, Nick, loved kids. He was already an uncle many times over through not only Nora, but his own two sisters and a brother, as well. "It wouldn't be for long."

"Overnight is too long." Kevin shook his head firmly. "Nick's still talking about us adopting and I don't want to give him more ammunition."

"Fine." But it wasn't fine at all. He'd done the right thing—saved his nephew from a mother who didn't deserve him, and now Adam had to come up with some answers. He couldn't think of anyone who might ride to the temporary rescue. Not as if he could ask his own ex-wife. Even the thought of that made him laugh quietly. Tricia was a TV reporter and had less knowledge of kids than he did. Besides that, he and Tricia hadn't spoken since their marriage ended more than five years ago. They'd had nothing in common then and even less now. And to top it all off, Tricia was working at a Seattle station now, so geographically undesirable anyway.

Frowning, Adam realized how insular his world was. He set his coffee cup down and tapped his fingers against the desktop. Most of the people he knew were business acquaintances. He didn't have time for friendships, so anyone he knew was just as busy as he was.

"You're tapping."

He stopped, looked at Kevin. "What?"

"Your fingers. Tapping. Either start playing a tune or cut it out."

"Right." Adam pushed to his feet and shoved both hands through his hair. "It shouldn't be this hard to figure out."

"What about Delores?"

Adam shook his head. "She's a housekeeper, not a nanny."

"But temporarily…"

"She leaves tomorrow to visit her sister in Ohio."

"Perfect."

"It's the beginning of summer. People take vacations." Of course, the reason his people were currently gone was because *he'd* bought them tickets. Was this some kind of weird Karma? Make him suffer for doing something nice for Anna Jameson and Delores Banner? It seemed like the universe itself was conspiring against him. And damned if Adam would surrender. There had to be someone—

As one particular thought sailed into his mind and settled in, Adam examined it from every angle.

Okay. It could work. If it didn't blow up in his face, first.

"Who are you thinking about?"

He looked at Kevin. "Sienna."

Kevin's mouth dropped open. "You want Devon's ex-wife to take care of Devon's kid with someone else."

Frowning, Adam murmured, "It didn't sound that bad in my head."

"Well it should have. Adam, she left Devon because he didn't *want* kids."

He waved that aside. "That's only one of the reasons."

"Exactly." Kevin stood up and faced his friend. "Devon was an ass to her and now you want to continue the Quinn family tradition?"

"This will be a straight-up business arrangement."

"Oh well, that's different then."

Ignoring the sarcasm, Adam stalked across the room to the wide window that overlooked the sea. Kevin was right, but that didn't matter because Adam couldn't think of anyone else *but* Sienna.

One part of his mind took in the scene before him, the impossibly small boat, red sails billowing in the wind. A pod of dolphins leaping from the water like ballet dancers. Surfers riding waves toward shore. But while he could enjoy the view, most of his brain was talking himself into his best chance. "She's the only one I know who could do this."

"Maybe, but why should she?" The argument was a good one and they both knew it. Kevin walked over to stand beside him. "When she divorced Devon, she didn't want his money. What makes you think she'll take yours?"

Adam looked at his oldest friend. "Because I won't give her a choice."

Sienna West gently tucked the newborn's arms beneath its chest, turned that perfect little face toward her, then stepped back and took the shot. The lighting was perfect. The pale, lemon yellow blanket beneath the baby highlighted the tiny girl's copper skin tone and the yellow-and-white daisies scattered around and across the impossibly small, naked body gave an almost fairy-like impression.

Sienna took a few more shots in rapid succession, then her assistant, Terri, stepped in to gently lay a daisy against the baby girl's ear. More clicks of the digital camera and finally Sienna sat back and smiled. She checked the screen on her camera and felt that familiar flush of accomplishment. They'd already been at it for half an hour while the baby quietly slept through prop changes, hair brushing and lighting changes. This couldn't last forever. Quickly, she scrolled through the shots, seeing ones she liked, ones she would edit and others she would delete.

Glancing up at the proud parents hovering close by, she said, "I think that's got it."

"They're going to be beautiful," the young mom said, hurrying in to scoop up her daughter and hold her close.

"Hard to be anything else," Sienna assured her. "She's a gorgeous baby."

"She is, isn't she?" the baby's father mused, reaching out to run one finger along his daughter's cheek.

Quickly, Sienna lifted her camera and took several shots of the family, connected, touching, sharing a moment they weren't even aware that they'd created. The tenderness of the young mother. The protective stance and gentle touch of the father and the sleeping baby nestled close. Checking her camera screen, Sienna smiled to herself. Since they hadn't asked for a family print, this would be a gift from her. And, with their permission, she'd showcase it on her website, as well.

Standing up, she said, "In about a week, I'll have some proofs to show you. Terri will give you the sign-in code for the website. Then all you have to do is decide which ones you want."

Kissing her baby tenderly, the mother laughed a little. "That's going to be the hard part, isn't it?"

"Usually, yes." Terri spoke up and began to herd the family from the room. "If you'll come with me, you can get Kenzie dressed and I'll get that code for you."

Sienna watched them go, then turned to her equipment. Terri was good with the clients. As the mother of four and grandmother of six, she knew her way around babies. Plus, she had a calming touch with nervous parents and jittery kids. Hiring her had been the best move Sienna had ever made.

She took the memory card from the camera, inserted it into the computer and opened a new folder for the Johnson family. Once the images were done loading, she flipped through them with a critical eye, deleting those that didn't meet her expectations and marking those that would be the winners.

Already, she loved the last-minute shots she'd taken of the family as a whole. It said something to her. The love in the mother's eyes. The trusting curl of the baby's body against her mother's chest. The protective gleam in the father's eyes and the visual element of his much bigger hand against his tiny daughter's cheek.

Sienna's heart gave a hard squeeze. Once upon a time, she'd dreamed of having kids herself. Of building a family with a man she loved, who would look at her and see everything in the world he wanted. She'd made a grab at the brass ring a few years ago—only to discover that she hadn't really caught it at all. Instead, she'd been grabbing at fog. Wisps of dreams that in the light of day lost all cohesion.

Devon Quinn had been both the dream and the nightmare. So handsome. So charming, with a wicked smile and a twinkle in his eyes that promised adventure and love. But she'd only seen what she'd wanted to see and it hadn't taken her long to figure out that marrying Devon had been the biggest mistake of her life. Now Sienna was divorced, with a struggling business taking pictures of children that weren't hers.

"Wow." Shaking her head, she ordered, "Snap out of it, Sienna."

She usually didn't wallow. Sienna was a firm believer in letting the past go and concentrating on the now. She didn't spend much time remembering Devon or the marriage that had been such a disappointment.

"Sienna?"

She looked up at Terri. "The Johnsons have a question?"

"No," the older woman said. "They paid and left. But someone else is here to see you."

Terri didn't look happy about it, either. Which only made Sienna wonder who could have put the uneasy look on her friend's face. "Who is it?"

"Me."

Terri jumped when the deep voice sounded out from right behind her. Sienna's gaze was locked on the man standing behind her assistant as she stood up slowly. Even if she hadn't seen him, she would have known that voice. Though she hadn't heard it in two years, she'd have recognized it anywhere. That voice was not just deep, it carried the ring of power, letting everyone know that the man speaking was used to being heard and obeyed.

Which just didn't fly with Sienna.

Still, her gaze locked with his and a rush of heat filled her stomach, swirled around for a heartbeat or two, then rose up in her chest.

Adam Quinn.

Her ex-brother-in-law. Funny, looking at Adam now, she could see the family resemblance between him and Devon. But she could see so much more than she once had. For example, Adam's chocolate eyes met hers squarely. They didn't shift around the room as Devon's had, as if he were looking for someone more interesting to talk to.

Adam's mouth was firm, and some would say grim, but Devon's smile, she'd discovered, was used to disarm, deceive. Adam's hair lacked the wave of Devon's, but somehow the expert, somewhat shaggy cut suited him. Devon had boasted a dark tan, which had come from so much time spent playing on lakes or ski slopes while Adam's skin was paler, letting her know that he was still more focused on his business than in entertaining himself.

He was taller than she remembered, Sienna thought. At least six foot two, and even wearing the elegantly tailored navy blue, three-piece suit, he looked more of a pirate than a businessman. Maybe, she told herself, it was because he carried an air of, not danger, exactly, but as if he were issuing a silent warning to stay out of his way or be mowed down.

And just watching him had her heartbeat speeding

up. It happened every time she was around Adam. Sienna hated acknowledging that, even to herself. Devon's brother was off-limits. Or should be. While Devon had been completely self-indulgent, Adam was too straitlaced. Too much the corporate raider for her. What she needed to do was find a man right in the middle of those two extremes. The problem was, Sienna didn't think she'd ever meet a man who could turn her insides into a blazing inferno with a single look like Adam could.

Two years since she'd spoken to him. Seen him. And the internal fire was sizzling away. Ridiculous or not, she really wished she were wearing something more flattering than a long-sleeved white shirt and an old pair of jeans.

When she realized the humming silence between them had been stretching out interminably, she cleared her throat. "Adam. What are you doing here?"

He stepped out from behind Terri and the woman sort of skittered sideways to keep out of his path. Sienna couldn't really blame her. Adam was intense.

"I need to talk to you," he said, slanting the other woman a look. "Privately."

Two

Giving orders again. Sienna shook her head. The man hadn't changed a bit. The last time she'd seen him, he'd begun their meeting by telling her exactly how to handle *her* divorce from his brother. He'd worked out a financial settlement that would have had most women flinging themselves at his manly chest, thanking him profusely. Instead, Sienna had told him what she'd told his brother. She didn't want the Quinn money. She just wanted the marriage to be over.

Now here he stood, two years later, still trying to take charge. Well, she'd hear him out, then go back to her life. The sooner she could put out the fire slowly boiling her blood, the better.

"Terri," she said, "would you mind?"

"Sure," the woman said, but added, "If you need me, I'll be right up front."

Sienna stopped her smile before it could get too big. Good to have friends. Even though the thought of the older woman trying to rescue her from Adam was ludicrous. "Thanks. I appreciate it."

Terri left, closing the door behind her. When she was gone, Adam asked, "What does she think I'm going to do?"

"Impossible to say," Sienna admitted. "But you do look scary and she has an excellent imagination."

"Scary?"

Well, she mused, he didn't look happy about that. "To someone who doesn't know you, yeah."

"So I don't scare you." He tucked his hands into his pockets and watched her, waiting for an answer.

"No, Adam. You don't." *But*, she added silently, *you worry me*.

"Good to know." Frowning, he glanced around what she called her "shoot room." While he looked, so did Sienna, seeing it as he did.

This was by no means her dream studio, but it would do for now. The images that came to life here shone when the building itself didn't. It was a plain room, really, the walls were a cool cream and unadorned. There were props stacked neatly on a series of shelves—everything from silly hats to baby blankets to old-fashioned slates that children scrawled their names on with chalk to be held in their photos. Right now, a sturdy table with the lemon yellow throw draped over a series of small pillows took up the middle of the set, with the lights focused down on where the baby had been lying. There was good light from the wide windows and when she had a night shoot, there were literally armies of lighting scaffolds scattered around the room.

Sienna studied him while he was unaware. To her, he looked way too good, and instinctively, she lifted her camera. Light and shadow played on his features, making him an irresistible target for her lens. In the late afternoon, she was losing the light, but there was enough to make him look almost dangerously alluring as he stood, half in shadow. She took two quick shots of him before he slowly swiveled his head to stare at her.

"I didn't come here to pose for you."

"I figured that. So why are you here, Adam?" She glanced down at the screen on her camera. Even the photo of him was hypnotic. Oh she was in bad shape.

"I need your help."

Surprised, she looked up at him. That, she hadn't expected. "Really? That's so unlike you."

His eyes narrowed. "Why?"

"You're just not the kind of man to ever ask for help."

"Know me that well, do you?"

"I think so," she said. As well as anyone could

know him, she hedged silently. Sienna was willing to bet that not even his ex-wife could claim to know him completely. Adam Quinn kept his thoughts and his feelings to himself. He had the best poker face in the universe and trying to see past the shields in his eyes could give you a migraine.

After she and Devon were married, she'd met Adam for the first time and thought then that two brothers couldn't have been more different. The fact that she'd also felt a quickening inside her for the quiet, stern-faced Adam was something that had embarrassed her at the time and was strangely even more mortifying now.

Tipping her head to one side, Sienna looked at him from across the room and wished she could flip the lighting on so his eyes wouldn't be in the shadows. "I was sorry to hear about Devon," she said abruptly, as a niggle of guilt pinged in the center of her chest. "I thought about calling you—after. But I didn't know what to say."

"Yeah." He pulled his hands from his pockets and reached down to pick up a tiny stuffed rabbit she'd used in the photo shoot with little Kenzie Johnson. He turned the soft, brown animal in his hands. "I get it. Devon didn't exactly treat you well."

Regret jabbed at her in twin stabs with the guilt. As much as she'd like to completely blame her failed marriage on her ex-husband, she just couldn't. Her mom always told her that it took two to make or break a marriage. So she had to accept her own share of the blame.

"It wasn't entirely Devon's fault," she said. "I wasn't what he wanted, either."

One eyebrow winged up. "Awfully generous."

"Not really," she said. "Just honest. What's going on, Adam? It's been two years since I've seen you, so why now?"

He tossed the little rabbit onto the table, then turned to face her dead-on. "I had a visit today from Devon's latest woman."

That news didn't even sting, which told Sienna as nothing else could have that she was truly over Devon Quinn. Heck, he'd had other women *while* they were married.

"And?"

"And," he said, reaching up to rub the back of his neck in a gesture of complete irritation. "She *sold* me Devon's son."

"She sold her child?" Sienna said it again because she could not believe what she was hearing. "And you *bought* him? You actually paid this woman for a *child*? Your own nephew?"

Adam stiffened and his features went even more grim. Eyes narrowed on her and she noticed a muscle in his jaw twitch as if he were grinding his teeth.

"I can't believe this. My God, Adam." She thought about little Kenzie Johnson and the love that had surrounded her. How her parents had practically beamed

with pride and adoration. She actually winced, thinking about Devon's son being sold off like a used car.
"You actually *bought* your nephew."

"What the hell choice did I have?" Adam sounded
furious and seemed to be asking himself the question
as well as her. He started pacing, in quick steps fu-
eled by rage. "Was I going to leave the boy with her?
Jesus, she hardly looked at him the whole time she
was negotiating." He snorted and repeated the word.
"No, she had a price, demanded it and waited for me
to pay it. It wasn't a negotiation. It was extortion."

Watching him quieted her own anger in sympathy for his. He'd lost his brother and then six months
later, his brother's only son had been held hostage by a
mercenary woman with her own agenda. Sienna was
almost too stunned to speak. Almost. The reality was
hard to get past. "She sold her child. Her own child."

A tiny ripple of pain washed through her. When
she'd married, she'd assumed that she and Devon
would have a family eventually. But that was one
of the things that had driven them apart. He'd flatly
refused, saying he didn't want kids slowing down
the "fun." He hadn't cared how Sienna felt about it.
His dismissal of her told her more than anything that
their marriage was doomed.

Now he'd made a child with a woman who clearly
didn't deserve or *want* the baby.

"Fifty thousand dollars." Adam snorted again, but
there was no humor there. Through gritted teeth, he

added, "Apparently *motherhood* was getting in the way of her career."

"You shouldn't have paid her a dime." What kind of woman would sell her own child? And what kind of man would pay her price?

His head snapped up and his gaze pinned hers. For a split second, Sienna felt a jolt of white-hot fury sizzle in the air between them. His expression was thunderous and maybe she should have been intimidated. But she wasn't. Maybe that expression worked on his employees, but not her. A second or two later, he seemed to understand that.

"What the hell else was I supposed to do?"

She threw her hands up. "Oh, I don't know. Have her arrested for trying to sell a baby? Take her to court? You've got legions of lawyers at your beck and call, and instead you wrote her a check."

He scrubbed both hands over his face and she could feel his frustration. "All I was thinking about was getting Devon's son away from her. This was the fastest solution."

Okay, she could see that, but her insides were still fisted and her heart pounding. "And what keeps her from coming back for more? For haunting that poor baby's life, constantly letting him know that he's nothing more to her than a bargaining chip?"

"I'm not an idiot," he snapped, firing a look at her that was designed to silence her arguments. "My lawyers wrote up a contract. She signed away her parental rights to me. I'm Jack's legal guardian now. God help us both."

Sienna blew out a breath. "Jack?"

"Yeah." He pushed one hand through his hair again and it occurred to Sienna she'd never seen Adam this *unsettled* before.

"Apparently," he continued, "Devon named his son for our father. And now the boy will never know either of them."

A twinge of sympathy for Devon, for Adam and mostly for the baby tugged at Sienna's heart. She'd thought when she left Devon that she was finished with the Quinn family. She'd made it a point to stay out of Adam's way over the last two years and that wasn't always easy. She and Adam didn't move in the same circles, of course. He was rich, powerful and she wasn't.

But she did take photos of the wealthy and famous. She did do photo spreads of some of the buildings he'd designed and built. But somehow, for two years, Sienna had managed to avoid him. Yet now, here he was, standing right in front of her.

She took a steadying breath that didn't really do the trick. "Fine. So the Mother of the Year took the money and ran, I'm guessing?"

"She was nothing but a blur when she hit the office door and she probably didn't stop until she got to the airport."

Disgusted, she muttered, "That's something, anyway."

Slanting her a look, he agreed. "Exactly how I feel about it."

She watched him as he wandered the room, looking at the props on the shelf, reaching out to pick up the wooden framed slate.

"So now what?" she asked.

He took a piece of chalk and scribbled something on the chalkboard while he talked. "That's why I'm here."

"Uh-huh. That doesn't tell me anything, Adam," she pointed out.

He flipped the slate around to her and Sienna read what he'd written.

I NEED A TEMPORARY NANNY.

She read it again, then lifted her gaze to his. "And you're telling me, why?"

"Because I need *you.*"

"Me?" Her brain was racing and her thoughts flew scattershot through her mind. Her? A nanny? For Devon's baby? What the hell? Shaking her head, she said, "I'm not a nanny, Adam. I'm a photographer with a growing business."

"I'm not asking you to give up your business."

"Sounds like you are."

"Look." He tossed the slate back onto the shelf, and then faced her. "I know this is weird, but damn it, Sienna, you're the only woman I know I can ask to do this."

"Oh come on." She laughed shortly and perched on the edge of a table. "You're hardly a monk, Adam. You know plenty of women."

"I know plenty of women who are great in my bed. Not so much with a small, defenseless human."

"I'm not quite sure how to take that," she admitted, even as her mind tried to settle down enough to figure it out. Naturally though, her brain went instead to images of Adam in bed. Naked. Not that she'd ever seen him naked, but Sienna had an excellent imagination.

"Take it as a compliment," he said tightly. He pushed one hand through his hair again and Sienna noted that the excellent cut meant his hair fell neatly back into place. She wondered if that idle gesture was done deliberately.

"Sienna," he said, releasing a long breath, "I know Devon treated you like crap and you have no reason to do any Quinn a favor—"

"Devon wasn't that bad, Adam," she interrupted him. "And I have nothing against you…"

To put it mildly. She had already been married to Devon when she met his older brother for the first time and Sienna hadn't been able to deny she felt a flash of something tantalizing the minute Adam had shaken her hand. And as her marriage crumbled, she'd often wondered what might have happened if she'd only met Adam first. But that was *not* the point at the moment.

"Good to know," he said, nodding. "I need you. That baby needs you."

She sucked in a gulp of air. "That was low."

"Yeah," he smiled briefly. "I know. But I learned a long time ago that you use whatever weapons you have to win the day."

He'd picked a good one to use on her was all Sienna could think. There was a reason most of her work centered around images of babies and children. "Great. That poor baby's a bargaining chip to his mother and a weapon to you."

"You know what I meant," he argued.

"Yes, I do." And she could see that he was really trying to do his best by his brother's child. Most men, she thought, would probably be trying to slip out of caring for the baby entirely. But that fact didn't make this any easier.

"Temporary, you said."

He nodded. "Just until we find someone permanent. You could help me with that. Pick out the right person."

"I don't know…" She looked around the room, at her equipment, the business she'd built from the ground up. If she did this, she'd be taking time away from the very thing that was most important to her.

But how could she *not* help care for a baby who'd really been given a lemon from the garden of mothers?

"I'll pay you whatever you want."

Sienna stiffened and lifted her chin as her gaze met his. "Just because you bought off the baby's mother doesn't mean that *every* woman is for sale. I don't want your money, Adam. I told you that when Devon and I divorced. I wouldn't take it from him. Didn't take it from you when you offered. Nothing's changed. I make my own way."

"Fine." He walked toward her, his eyes flashing as he stared at her. "I respect that. Admire it even. But I can't be in your debt like this, either, Sienna. So instead of paying you, why don't I help you with your career?"

She laughed shortly. "How do you plan to do that? Pose for me, after all?"

"No." He came closer. Close enough that Sienna was forced to tip her head back to meet his dark brown eyes. His scent came to her and she noted it was just like him. Subtle, rich and tempting. She held her breath.

"Your studio's a little on the small side," he mused, giving a quick, assessing glance around the space.

Insulted, she argued, "It works just fine."

His gaze snapped back to hers. "You should never settle for 'fine,' Sienna."

"I don't plan to. I'll get something bigger one day."

"Why wait?" He gave a shrug that was deliberately careless, but she didn't believe it for a minute.

"What?" He couldn't be saying what she thought he was saying.

"Here's the deal. You help me out with the baby—"

"Stop calling him 'the baby,'" she interrupted. "You said his name is Jack."

"All right. Help me with *Jack* and you'll get your dream studio out of it."

"Adam—"

"You find the building you want," he continued, steamrolling over whatever argument she might have made. "And my company will take care of the rest. We'll rehab, remodel, set it all up to your specifications."

Her heart was pounding. His words hung in the air like helium party balloons, bright, pretty. Her studio now was small, but she'd been saving her money, building her reputation. The long-term plan was to have a higher-end studio that would draw bigger clients. Eventually, she dreamed of being the top photographer in Huntington Beach, California, maybe even on the whole West Coast.

And if she did this for Adam, that could happen a lot faster. God, she was so tempted. But if she did this...

"What?" he demanded. "You're thinking and they're not good thoughts."

Irritated, she muttered, "Stop trying to read my mind."

"Don't really have to try when whatever you're thinking or feeling is stamped all over your face."

"Well that's insulting." And unsettling.

"Didn't mean it that way."

She waved one hand at him. "I was just thinking…if I do this, would I be any better than Jack's mother? She used him for profit. Wouldn't I be doing the same thing?"

"No." One word. Flat. Final.

She looked into his eyes and saw that he meant it. Too bad it didn't convince *her*.

"You're nothing like her, Sienna." He paused. "Hell. No one is. If you do this, it's not about Jack at all. It's a favor to *me*."

God help her, she was wavering. Shaking her head, she continued her argument against doing this by saying softly, "I have a job, Adam. And I can't take a baby along with me on photo shoots."

"I understand and we'll work it out. I don't know how yet, but I'll find a way."

He would, too. Nothing stopped Adam Quinn from doing whatever it was he wanted to. According to Devon, his older brother was a human bulldozer, plowing down everything in his path. Once, she'd thought Devon was like that, too. She'd met him and seen ambition where there was only charisma. She'd thought him charming but hadn't realized the charm was practiced and not at all genuine.

Adam, on the other hand, clearly didn't care a damn about charm. He was practically a force of nature. He'd come here for the express purpose of getting Sienna's help no matter what it took and he was very close to succeeding. Adam didn't need Devon's easy smile or quick wit. He had the power of his personality going for him. He was absolutely up-front about what he wanted and how he was going to get it and that could be hard to take even if it was safer in the long run.

"I'm not asking you to give up your work," he said. "Hell, I'm offering to give you a dream studio so you can build your business faster than you would have been able to. I just need some temporary help."

His mouth screwed up as if even the word *help* left a bad taste in his mouth. This was not a man accustomed to needing anyone.

"In exchange," he added a moment later, "I'll give you the best photography studio in California."

He'd laid her dreams out for her on a silver platter. They were right there, within reach and Sienna felt a little light-headed at the prospect. She wanted it. Fine, she could admit it, to herself at least, that she really wanted a beautiful, state-of-the-art studio. She could build the career she'd dreamed of with the right tools. And if she didn't take Adam's deal it could take her years to earn that reality on her own.

This was a bad idea, though. There was history

between them, not to mention the ghost of his dead brother. She didn't want to be attracted to him but she most definitely *was*. And as that thought skittered through her mind, she deliberately kept her features blank. She really didn't need him reading her expression at the moment.

He was watching her and Sienna fought to keep what she was feeling off her face. Now that she knew he was reading her expressions, it put her at a real disadvantage. But how could her mind *not* wander to his broad chest, his deep brown eyes, his strong hands? *Oh God.* One corner of his mouth lifted briefly as if he knew what she was trying to do.

So she took a breath and got it over with. "Okay, I'll do it. But—"

"Great." He pushed his sleeve back, glanced at the heavy platinum watch on his wrist, then looked at her. "What time are you finished here today?"

"Just hold on a second. We need to talk about a few things and—"

"We will," he said quickly. "Later. So, when can you leave?"

"Uh—" If he kept cutting her off in an attempt to hurry this arrangement along, she'd never be able to say what she needed to. She had a few ground rules of her own to lay down and she knew he wouldn't be happy to hear them. But the man was like the tide, pushing inexorably toward shore. No point in arguing with him here. "Fine. I can leave in about an hour."

"Good. That'll work. I'll meet you at your house, help you move your stuff to my place."

She blinked at him. "You'll what? I'm sorry. *What?*" She shook her head as if to clear her hearing.

"If you're going to take care of the baby, you'll have to be where he is, right?" He looked at her steadily and his gaze was strong enough that she felt the power of the man slide into her.

That hadn't occurred to her at all and now she had to wonder *why*. Of course she'd have to be with the baby to take care of him. But she just hadn't put that together with living in Adam's house. And now that she was, Sienna was pretty sure this was a bad idea.

"I didn't think I'd be living with you."

"Not with me. At the same address."

"Oh." She nodded and shrugged. "Sure. That's a whole different thing."

He blew out a breath at her sarcasm and that told her he was a lot closer to the edge of exasperation than she'd thought. "It's a big house, Sienna. You'll have your own suite."

Her eyebrows arched. A suite? *Not the point, Sienna.* "I don't know…"

"Remember our deal. You find any building you want, Sienna. You can design the remodel yourself."

The snake in the garden had probably sounded a lot like Adam Quinn.

"Put in shelves and workrooms and prop rooms and any kind of lighting you need."

She ignored the inner tug she felt toward that tasty carrot he was holding out in front of her. He knew all too well that he was getting to her. And she imagined her expression told him everything he wanted to know. "You're still selling me on an idea I already agreed to. Feeling a little desperate, Adam?"

For a second she thought he'd deny it, then he clearly thought better of it.

"Not quite," he admitted. "But it's close. Look, Sienna, we can help each other here. That's it. So are you in or not?"

She met his gaze for a long second or two. She could say no, but why should she? There was a baby who needed to be cared for and a man completely out of his depth asking for her help.

And okay, the photography studio.

But there was another reason to do it. One she didn't really want to think about. It was Adam, himself. It was his eyes. The deep timbre of his voice. And the way he looked at her. Foolish? Probably. Irresistible? Absolutely.

"Okay," she said before she could talk herself out of it. "I'm in."

Relief flashed across his features briefly. "Good. That's good. So I'll meet you at your place in two hours. Help you move what you need to my house."

"Okay." Decision made, her stomach was still spinning. She'd have to get her neighbors to watch the house and bring in the mail and— "I'll write down my address."

"I know where you live."

She looked up at him. "You do?"

His gaze locked on hers. "I've always known, Sienna."

Three

Two hours later, as promised, Adam pulled up in front of a small bungalow in Seal Beach and parked beneath the shade of an ancient tree. A hell of a day. He had a headache that pounded hard enough to shatter his skull and it didn't look as if it would be going away anytime soon.

Staring at the house, Adam frowned a little. Bright splashes of color lined the front of the house, flowers spilling out of the beds onto a lawn that hadn't been mowed in a while. The paint was faded and the roof looked as old as the tree.

"Why the hell would she refuse a settlement when she divorced Devon?" he wondered aloud. There was a place for pride—no one understood that better than he did. But damn it, pride shouldn't get in the way of common sense. Clearly, she could have used the money.

The street the house sat on was old and settled. Most of the houses were small, but well kept. A crowd of kids across the street were playing basketball against a garage and the throaty roar of a lawn mower sounded in the distance. He tapped his fingers against the steering wheel and glanced at Sienna's faded green sedan parked in her driveway. The rusted bumper irritated him more than he could say.

"Hardheaded woman," he muttered. "She should have taken Devon for millions."

Climbing out of his car, he walked up to the house, noting the cracks in the sidewalk, the chipping stucco alongside the garage door. Grinding his teeth together, he made a dozen mental notes on the short walk to the porch. They had a deal, but he was adding to it whether she liked it or not. His company would give her the best damn photography studio in the state, but they would also redo this house. And if she argued with him about it—which she would— he'd steamroll right over any objections she came up with.

Sienna had married his brother and Devon had proven quickly just what a bad decision that had been. Adam couldn't ignore his family's mistakes. He'd fix them if he could, and this he could definitely take care of. By the time he was finished with this tiny house, Sienna would think she was living in a damn palace.

She answered the door before he'd had a chance to knock, which told Adam she'd been watching for his arrival. Her eyes were wide and her expression wary. Had she changed her mind? Was she going to try to back out of their deal? If so, she would fail.

"You don't look happy to see me," he mused.

"Stop reading my mind."

He laughed shortly. "Well, that was honest anyway."

"That's not what I meant. I mean, of course, I'm happy to see you. Well, not happy, but I was expecting you and—" She stopped, scowled and took a deep breath. Once she'd released it again, she started over.

"Hi, Adam."

"Hi." He liked knowing that he made her nervous. Liked that she got a gleam in her eyes when she looked at him. He knew that same gleam was in his own eyes every time he saw her. How could it not be? Tall and curvy, with those big blue eyes, Sienna was enough to bring most men to their knees.

She pushed the screen door wider for him, then turned back into the house as he stepped inside.

His gaze swept the interior quickly, with a professional eye that missed almost nothing. Inside at least, the house appeared to be in better shape than the exterior. The walls were jewel toned, a deep scarlet in the living room, fading to a soft rose in the hall. He could only imagine what the rest of the house looked like, but realized he was curious about her home. About her.

The old, scuffed wooden floors had been polished and she had what looked like fifties-style braided rugs in a variety of colors spread throughout the hall and the front room. Her furniture wasn't new or contemporary but it suited her. There were framed prints of photos on the walls. Her work, he imagined. Seascapes, meadows, people and, for some reason, babies dressed up like flowers and fruit.

She followed his gaze and grinned. "They're so cute when they're tiny—it's fun to dress them up."

"Sure." He shook his head, studying one baby in particular. "What is that? A peach?"

"Yes."

"Hmm." He shrugged and looked at her. "I like the beach scenes."

"Thanks."

"We've actually got a new building going up down in Dana Point," he said thoughtfully. "Sits above the beach and it's a different kind of design."

"Really?"

It was easy enough to see how intrigued she was, so Adam kept talking. The idea had only just occurred to him, but now that it had, he went with it. "The architect really outdid herself. The building is a curve of glass that faces the ocean, but there are open areas all over the face of it, too."

"What do you mean?"

"Sort of mini balconies, I guess you'd call them," he said, staring again at one of her framed seascapes. "There will be some kind of ivy trailing on the railings so that the whole thing will give the impression of the building itself growing out of the land." He could see it now, in his head, as he could every project he'd ever done. Adam liked doing projects that challenged him. That worked his imagination as much as his skills. "With the sky and the ocean reflecting off the glass panels, it will make the trails of ivy even more alive, I think."

"Wow."

One word, spoken in a kind of hush. Adam looked at her. "What?"

Smiling, she shook her head and said, "I've just never heard you talk like that. I mean, you're obviously good at what you do, but—"

"But most buildings these days are fairly boring?" he asked, one corner of his mouth tipping up. "Sort of generic."

"Well, yes." She led the way into the living room and he looked around as he followed her.

More framed prints here. His gaze swept them, empty beaches, lonely people, cheerful babies. Each one was perfectly lit, with shadows sliding in giving them all a depth they might not have had otherwise.

But he had to wonder if she was aware of just how much of *herself* was displayed on her walls.

"I don't mean they're not beautiful, but this project you're talking about sounds amazing."

He nodded. "It will be, once it's finished. But now I realize I'd like some pictures taken during the process of building."

"So you want a before, during and after series?"

"I guess so. Interested?"

Her eyes lit up and he was glad he'd asked her, just to see that brightness fill her eyes. "Absolutely. Yes."

"Okay, in a day or two, we'll take a ride down Pacific Coast Highway so I can show you around."

"Good." She nodded. "That's good."

She was close, Adam realized. Standing so close to him, he inhaled her scent with every breath. Her eyes caught his and held and Adam felt a throbbing tension erupt between them. He read her expression easily and knew she was feeling the same thing. For a long second, he stared down at her and fought the urge to pull her in close and—

Yeah. Don't go there. "You ready?"

"Yes. At least, I think I've got everything," she said, grabbing up a lightweight jacket off a nearby chair.

His eyebrows lifted as he looked at the duffel bag and a small, wheeled suitcase sitting beside the front door. "That's it?"

She looked too, then turned to meet his gaze. "Yes, why?"

Chuckling, he said, "Most of the women I know take more luggage than *that* for an overnight trip. I don't even want to think about what they'd be hauling for two weeks."

She grinned and a ball of fire flashed instantly to life in his gut. It was all too familiar to him. From the moment they'd first met, Adam had felt that jolt of something hot and dangerous. Naturally, he'd kept it on a tight leash, since she was his brother's wife. Then when Devon and Sienna divorced, Adam had kept his distance because he'd figured she'd had enough of the Quinn family to last a lifetime.

Now here he was, taking her to his home. If he couldn't find a way past the hard tug of desire, it was going to be a *long* couple of weeks. He would handle it, though. That's what Adam did. When faced with a situation, he found a way through it, or around it. And if there was one thing Adam was good at, it was focusing. That's all he had to do. *Focus.* Not on what he wanted, but on what he needed. And damn it, he needed Sienna's help.

"Adam?" she asked, dropping one hand onto his forearm. "Are you okay?"

"Yeah. I'm fine." A light, friendly touch, and yet, it felt like lightning striking between them. She felt it too because she let her hand fall away. Brusquely, he stepped back from her. Distance would be key, he told himself. Best to stop now. "You're sure this is it."

"If I need something else, I can always come back here to get it. Not like I'm going to the other side of the country." She smiled again. "Besides, I'm not like most women. I travel light."

And a part of him was impressed by that. The women who came and went from his life were interchangeable in their attitudes toward clothes, jewelry and being in the right place at the right time. After a while, they all seemed to be practically clones of each other. None of them were interested in anything beyond the next society function or charity fundraiser. They didn't even care what the charity was for. It was mainly a chance to see and be seen and it bored Adam beyond the telling of it.

He couldn't imagine Sienna bothering to put on makeup before she so much as left her bedroom in the morning. Hell, all she was wearing now as far as he could tell, was a little mascara and some lip gloss. And damned if she wasn't the most beautiful thing he'd seen in a long time.

"You really didn't have to come pick me up," she was saying, and Adam paid attention. "I've got my own car and I remember where your house is."

"I don't know," he mused. "*Car* is a pretty generous description of what's parked out in your driveway. I doubt you'd have made it all the way to Newport."

His home in Newport Beach was fourteen miles from Seal Beach, but as far as neighborhoods went, it might as well be light-years from here. Adam frowned at that random thought and wondered when the hell he'd become a snob.

"Hey." Insulted, she insisted, "Gypsy is a great car."

"Gypsy?" he snorted. "You named your car?"

"Don't you?" She shook her head as she swung a giant brown leather purse onto her shoulder, then wheeled the suitcase closer.

"No."

Now she shrugged. "Cars are people, too. We yell at them, bargain with them—'please don't run out of gas here'—why shouldn't they have names?"

"That is possibly," Adam said thoughtfully, "the weirdest argument I've ever heard."

"Think about it the next time your car doesn't start and you're cursing it."

"My cars *always* start."

"Of course they do." She laughed. "No adventure in that, is there?"

"Adventure?" This was the strangest conversation he'd ever had with a woman. And Adam realized that he was enjoying himself more than he had in a long time.

"Well sure," she said. "If everything goes right all the time, where's the fun in that?"

"I don't consider a car breaking down to be fun."

"It can be." She dug in the oversize bag and came out with a set of keys. "The last time my fan belt snapped, I found the greatest bakery/coffee shop. I waited for AAA there and had an amazing slice of German chocolate cake."

"Fascinating." And she was. Not only did her looks appeal to him, but the way her mind worked intrigued him.

"You just never know. One time I got a flat tire and took the most amazing sunset pictures." She sighed a little as if remembering. "I was on my way to an appointment and never would have seen it if I hadn't been forced to stop."

So, in Sienna's world, a flat tire or a snapped fan belt was a *good* thing. "You're an interesting woman."

Her smile brightened. "Isn't that a nice thing to say?"

A laugh shot from his throat, surprising them both. "Only you would find a compliment in there."

"I'd much rather be interesting than boring," she quipped. "So maybe you're hanging out with the wrong women."

"Maybe I am," he admitted. Hell, he hadn't laughed with a woman in far longer than he liked to think about.

She tipped her head to one side and her blond hair swept out in a golden fall. A smile teasing her mouth, she looked up at him. "There may be hope for you, Adam."

His gaze locked with hers. "Hope for what?"

"Well," she countered, "that's the question, isn't it?"

His body stirred and his mind filled with all kinds of things he might hope for. Then he got control again and reminded himself that no matter how much he wanted her, Sienna West was off-limits. "Is every conversation with you going to be this confusing?"

"If we're lucky." Still smiling, she lifted her suitcase.

"I'll get that."

"Nope. You can carry the bag with my clothes. Nobody carries my cameras but me."

"Cameras? Plural?" he asked, looking at the rolling suitcase. "How many do you need?"

"Well I don't know, do I?" she said patiently. "That's why I bring a selection."

The tone in her voice was patient, as if she were talking to a three-year-old. Irritating. Amazing how quickly she could turn what he was feeling from attraction to annoyance. And it would be best all the way around if he just *stayed* annoyed. "Right."

"And remember, I'll be going to work when I have to, Adam." She looked up at him. "You already agreed to that. I've got four appointments this week."

He nodded. Safe ground. Hell, he was willing to compromise. After all, the baby wasn't really *her* responsibility. No, little Jack Quinn was now Adam's charge. Just for a second or two, Adam's legendary self-confidence wavered. He knew next to nothing about raising children. Hadn't exactly had prime role models in his own parents. He'd be feeling his way through this blind, but he was determined to succeed.

Devon's son deserved a happy life and Adam was going to see to it that the kid got exactly that. "Not a problem. We'll work around your appointments."

"Okay, good." Nodding, she turned to lock the front door, then started down the front steps.

"I appreciate this, Sienna." He frowned briefly. Adam wasn't accustomed to being so damn humble and he realized it left a bad taste in his mouth. Asking for assistance was just out of his normal world. He did what needed doing. He was the one in charge. Finding answers, solving problems. Now everything was different. "In case you were unaware, I'm not used to having to ask for help."

"Yeah, I got that," she said. "But everyone needs help sometimes."

"Not me," he muttered, then said louder, "Look, I realize this might be…awkward. You. Devon's child."

Sienna held up one hand and shook her head. "Don't. Don't read things into this that aren't there. It's not like that for me. So we should probably get this out of the way right from the jump. Devon and

I were divorced two years ago. And it was over for me for at least a year before that."

Her voice was soft, but her eyes flashed, letting him know that this was important to her. That she wanted him to not just listen but to *hear* her.

"I'm sorry Devon died. I really am. But not for my own sake, Adam. For you. For your mom." She reached out and laid one hand on his forearm. "I'm happy to help with the baby, but I'm not hurt that he had a child with someone else. Devon and I were much better friends than we were a couple. I'm not a victim, Adam. I'm doing fine on my own."

He studied her for a long minute before nodding. "Okay, yeah. I can see that you are. I'm glad for that. It will make things easier on all of us."

"Good." She gave him a quick smile. "We'd better get going. I'll just follow you."

Frowning again, Adam countered, "I was going to give you a ride to the house."

"And without a car, I'll get to work how?" Shaking her head, she said, "Nope. I need Gypsy, so I'll follow you. And don't worry about losing me. Like I said, I remember where you live."

He didn't like the idea of her driving what looked like a hunk of metal held together with prayer. The damn car was an accident waiting to happen. But one look into her eyes told him if he said anything, he'd have a battle on his hands.

Ordinarily, Adam wasn't against a good battle;

nothing he liked better than getting into the middle of a debate and proving just how right he was. But today, he didn't have time for it. Once she was at his house, he'd take care of the car situation. He had half a dozen cars at his place; she could take her pick of them. Hell, he'd make it part of their deal if he had to. She'd go for it.

"Fine," he said, willing to let it go for now.

"So is Delores watching the baby at the house?"

"Just for tonight. She's going on vacation tomorrow." He carried her out to the drive. "Kevin drove the baby to the house."

She laughed and the sound lifted into the air and hung there like a rainbow shining through gray clouds. Turning to grin up at him, she repeated, "Kevin? How'd you talk him into that?"

"He works for me."

"Uh-huh." She waited, watching him knowingly.

Finally, Adam sighed. "I'm buying lunch for the rest of the month."

"Oh. Good bribe."

"I don't bribe people—" He stopped and nodded. "I incentivize." When she didn't say anything, he admitted, "Fine. It was a bribe."

"So, how is Kevin? He and Nick still together?"

"Yeah. They got married a year ago."

"That's great," she said. "Did Nick ever open the restaurant he was always talking about?"

Adam carried her bag to the back of her car. "He

went into catering instead. Decided it was less frustrating to deal with one picky client than an entire restaurant of customers. His place is called Tonight's the Night."

"Oh, I like it."

"Yeah, he's doing really well."

She walked straight to her car, stabbed the key into the trunk lock and—nothing. "Come on, baby, just open up…"

"Let me try," Adam said, taking the keys from her.

Sienna tried to snatch them back, but Adam evaded her.

"I can do it," she argued. "It just sticks sometimes, that's all."

"Right." Adam tried the key himself with the same results. Scowling, he tried a few more times before crying defeat. "Yes, this is the car you want to depend on."

"There's nothing wrong with my car." She grabbed the keys, walked to the driver's side and opened the passenger door. Carefully, she set the suitcase on the backseat, then motioned for him to hand over her duffel bag. When he did, she tossed it inside as well and closed the door. "See? Everything's fine."

"Except you can't open the trunk."

"Turns out, I didn't need to."

"Are you this stubborn with everyone? Or just me?"

"Everyone."

"Great."

"Now, if we're finished dissing Gypsy…" She gave the car a pat, then opened the driver's door. "I'll meet you at your place."

"Just follow me." It was an order, not a request.

"Sure."

She'd already dismissed him, climbing into her car and firing up the so-called engine that coughed and hacked like a tuberculosis patient. Leaning down, he peered into the window. "Straight down PCH, past Fashion Island to—"

"Adam, I *know.*" Shaking her head, she asked, "Honestly, are you this bossy with everyone? Or is it just me?"

Frowning as she tossed his words back at him with a twist, he grumbled, *"Everyone."*

"I actually knew that." She grinned and shoved the gear stick into Reverse.

He bit back his frustration and turned for his own car. Once inside, he fired up the engine, then made a U-turn and waited to make sure she followed him. Hell, to make sure her vehicle could keep up. He didn't trust that rusted-out piece of junk she was driving.

Sienna was irritating, attractive and hardheaded enough that he could only think that the next two weeks were going to be a nightmare. Especially because he wanted her now more than he ever had. What Adam couldn't understand was why arguing with Sienna left him more intrigued than a polite conversation with anyone else. Aggravated with himself, he deliberately pushed all thoughts of Sienna out of his mind for the rest of the drive.

Fifteen minutes later, Adam turned off Pacific Coast Highway and waited for Sienna to catch up. Cars had moved in and out of the space between them like blips in a video game, but she shouldn't be more than a minute or two behind him.

He waited. Five minutes. Ten. Then grumbling, turned his car around and backtracked, looking for her. "That fossil she's driving probably broke down and she's waiting for a rescue," he told himself. "Well if she'd listened to me in the first place—"

It wasn't long before he spotted her car parked on PCH not far from the Huntington Pier. She wasn't in the car. And she wasn't standing beside it, looking for her rescuer.

"Of course." Adam blew out a breath as he drove past her. Turning around as soon as he could, he parked behind her so-called car, got out and walked to find her.

The wind whipped past him, rushing inland, carrying the scent of the sea along with it. The palm trees danced in the wind like chorus girls in a Vegas review and a froth of foam dotted the waves headed toward shore. And there was Sienna—crouched at the edge of the greenbelt, holding her camera to her eye, focusing on the ocean and the surfers gliding on their boards.

He studied her for a second or two, admiring her complete concentration, her focus. She was unaware of him or anything else that wasn't outlined in the center of her camera lens. Her blond hair waved like a flag in the wind and the faded jeans she wore cupped her behind lovingly. He took a breath and deliberately looked away from that particular view.

"What're you doing?"

Sienna didn't even glance at him and that fried his ass just a bit. "I'm taking some pictures."

"And you had to stop to do this now?"

"Had to capture the light on the waves," she said, not answering the question at all.

He glanced out to where her camera was pointed. "Yeah. Sunlight. Happens every day."

Now she did swivel her head to look up at him. There was a mixture of pity and exasperation in her eyes. "You have no vision."

It wasn't her words so much as the expression in her gaze that slapped at him. "My vision's good enough."

"Is it?" She turned away to take a few more pictures, the quiet, repetitive click of the shutter the only sound between them. Finally, though, she stood up and looked him in the eye. "You see what you have to see, Adam. What you expect to see. Anything that isn't on your agenda gets overlooked."

"Because I don't daydream while driving or get distracted from the task at hand, that makes me what? A barbarian?"

She laughed and shook her head. "No, it just makes you...*you*."

"Glad to hear it," he snapped, though he had a feeling he'd just been insulted. But he wasn't dealing with it now.

"What I *expected* to see was your pitiful car right behind me."

Her mouth twitched once, then she sobered again. "Well, I'm finished now, so we can go."

Adam was torn. He admired a strong will and a woman with the strength to go toe-to-toe with him. But he also wanted to set the tone for this arrangement. He would be the one calling the shots, whether she liked it or not, so she'd better get used to the idea.

"Before we go—"

"Yes?" Her hair twisted in the wind and she shook it back from her face.

"When you're watching the baby I expect your 'vision' to be focused on him."

"What's that supposed to mean?"

"It seems pretty clear to me." He shrugged. "You were supposed to be following me and instead you detoured to do something else entirely." He shoved his hands into his pockets and flicked a quick glance at the sea. "I don't want that happening around Jack."

"You really think I would?" Insult colored her words and a dangerous glint flashed in her eyes.

"I didn't say that."

"You did everything but."

"Then you agree I didn't say it."

She took a deep breath, closed her eyes and a second later said, "Nine, ten." She opened her eyes and fixed her gaze on his. "Look, Adam. I agreed to help you out and that's just what I'm going to do, but you're not going to micromanage me while I do it."

"I'm not?" Amused now, he gave her a half smile that disappeared again an instant later.

"No, because if you can't agree to back off, I won't do it at all."

"You already agreed."

"And I keep my word," she said, then added, "unless provoked."

He could argue the point with her. Because when it came to provocation, he had more to complain about than she did. They could stand there beside the palm tree that continued to sway with the wind and talk circles around each other until late into the night. But the bottom line was, he *needed* her. So for now, he'd give her this point. But he'd manage anything in his own damn house that he wanted to manage and there wouldn't be a thing she could do about it. Because he *knew* Sienna West. She would never walk away from a baby who needed her. No matter the provocation.

"You'll be provoked," he said, not even sure himself if it was a warning or a promise. "Clearly," he added, "so will I."

"Are you irritated? Again?"

"The feeling's becoming alarmingly familiar," he admitted. "And we both know you won't back out on a deal."

Her blue eyes were squinted against the afternoon sunlight as she turned to look out at the sea. The first hints of sunset were staining the cloud-spattered sky, lavender, pink, deep gold. While she took her sweet time answering him, Adam studied her. Her profile was sharp and strong. Her blond hair whipped around her face and lifted into the same wind that plastered her white, button-down shirt against her body, defining her high, full breasts to such a degree that Adam had to curl his hands into fists to keep from reaching for her.

His body tightened, his heartbeat jumped into a gallop and he told himself that if he was as smart as he thought he was, he'd call this whole thing off. Having this woman in his home for at least the next couple of weeks and not being able to have her was going to be torture.

One stray thought slid through his brain. *His brother had been an idiot.*

Adam wouldn't make the same mistakes. Devon had married Sienna, and then let her leave. Adam wasn't going to be involved with her at all, because if he allowed that, he'd never let her go. And he'd already proven that he sucked at relationships.

So Sienna was off-limits.

Damn it.

"I said I'd stay and I will," she told him flatly. "But, Adam, you make the decisions for the baby. You don't make *mine*."

"Agreed." With reservations, he added silently. If he saw something that needed doing then he'd damn well arrange for it to happen.

Whether Sienna West liked it or not.

Four

Adam's house was as spectacular as Sienna remembered.

She followed his car through the scrolled ironwork gate along the drive edged with flowers and trees, and then parked beside him. She got out of the car and took a moment to let her gaze slide across the house and grounds.

The house itself was Tuscan style, with lots of aged brick, cream-colored stucco and heavy wood shutters at every window. Along the second story was a balcony with a black iron railing and terracotta pots boasting rivers of flowers in bright colors that spilled onto the deck. It sat high on a hill above

Newport Beach, boasting an amazing view of the ocean and the bay, where hundreds of luxury boats dipped and swayed in their berths.

The entry, she remembered, was a long, tiled walkway lined with arches adorned by bougain-villea vines in rich shades of red, purple and coral. The yard was a wide sweep of meticulously tended green dotted by trees along a high wall separating the estate from the street.

It was perfect—and to her photographer's eye, a dream house, begging to be documented.

"You ready for this?" Adam was right beside her and she hadn't heard him move.

He was so close she swore she could feel heat pouring from his body to wrap itself around her. And in spite of that warmth, or maybe because of it, she shivered a little.

"I'm ready," she said, swallowing hard before turning her head to meet his gaze. "It's just two weeks, Adam. What could happen?"

One corner of his mouth lifted and Sienna took a quick breath. The man was so damn confident al-ready, she didn't need to let him know that his slight-est smile was enough to make her knees quiver.

"That's what we're going to find out, Sienna." He turned to open her car door. "I'll get your stuff."

She was grateful he wasn't looking at her face at the moment. If he read her expression now, Adam would know exactly how much he affected her. And that was one secret she didn't want to share.

"I'll get the cameras," she reminded him. Idle daydreaming over gorgeous homes was over. Now it was time to begin the bargain that would open the way to her creating her own dreams. She took the bag with her cameras and Adam grabbed the duffel, then led her toward the house.

"I called Delores to let her know we were coming."

"How is she?" Sienna remembered the older woman as warm and friendly. Of course, that was when Sienna and Devon were married. There was no telling how the woman would react to her now.

"Same as always," he said, not bothering to look back at her. "Like I told you before, tomorrow she's leaving to visit her sister in Ohio for two weeks, which is why I need the help."

Reminder: It would be just her, Adam and the baby in the beautiful house for the next two weeks. Her stomach did a quick dip and spin at the thought and a treacherous tingle set up shop just a little lower. Oh, this could be really bad.

Keeping a tight grip on her suitcase, Sienna followed Adam down that beautiful entry and through the double, hand-carved doors. To avoid watching him, she shifted her gaze to take in the interior of the house. It was even more impressive than the outside and that was saying something.

Wide, rust-colored tiles swept through the entire first

floor, with huge, floral rugs in faded shades of blues and greens offering warmth. The ceilings were open beamed and every wall boasted floor-to-ceiling windows to take advantage of the ocean views. The furniture was heavy and oversize, but comfortable and seemed to set a welcoming tone in a place that would otherwise have felt intimidating by its sheer size and opulence.

A red-tiled staircase swept off the entryway in a wide curve accompanied by hand-carved wooden banisters. She knew the bedrooms were upstairs because she and Devon had stayed here a couple of times. And she knew the views from the second story would take her breath away.

"There you are!" A woman's voice carried to them, followed by the smart clip of heels against the floor.

Sienna turned to watch Delores Banner walk into the room, a beautiful baby perched on her hip. Delores was about fifty, with graying blond hair that swung around her face in a long bob. Her eyes were blue and her mouth was curved in a smile.

"Sienna. It's good to see you again."

A small wave of relief swept through Sienna at the other woman's greeting. She'd been half-afraid that she might somehow blame Sienna for what had happened to Devon. Which made Sienna wonder if there wasn't a small part of herself that felt blame, too. Silly of course. She'd had nothing to do with Devon's death. They'd divorced two years before he died, but maybe guilt was harder to let go of than she would have thought.

"Thank you, Delores. Good to see you, too." But it was the baby on the woman's hip who had Sienna's attention. She set her suitcase of equipment down carefully and walked across the room. "This must be Jack."

The baby looked up at her with big golden-brown eyes and a smile tugging at his mouth. His dark brown hair stood up in tufts and a dimple winked in one cheek. Sienna's heart melted.

"The image of his daddy, isn't he?" Delores bounced a little, making the baby chortle and wave both hands. Shaking her head, she looked at Sienna. "Such a shame. Devon will never—" She stopped talking abruptly, lifted her chin and said, "Never mind that. It's good of you to take care of him while I'm gone, Sienna. I swear if my sister hadn't made so many plans, I'd cancel."

"You're not going to cancel anything," Adam said in a tone that brooked no argument. "We'll be fine without you for two weeks. Sienna will be here and she's going to help me find a nanny, too."

"There he goes again," Delores said to Sienna, then turned a heated gaze on her employer. "I told you we don't need a nanny. I'm perfectly capable of taking care of this baby."

"And when you want to visit your sister again?" Adam asked.

"Well—"

"Why don't you let me hold him?" Sienna reached out and scooped little Jack into her arms. Instantly the tiny boy patted her face and smiled.

He was small but sturdy and had that special smell that all babies seemed to have. Something soft and innocent that made Sienna want to cradle him close and protect him from the world. While Jack played with her twist of silver earrings, she listened in on the argument between Delores and Adam. Fascinated, she admired the housekeeper even more than she had before. Not many people could stand up to Adam Quinn without blinking.

Delores countered, "We can work something out or my sister can visit me here until Jack's older…"

"Delores." Adam frowned at her. "It's not your job to deal with the baby."

"So you don't trust me to do it?"

"I didn't say that."

"Then I can do it."

"I didn't say that, either."

"I don't know what you're saying, or not, but I'll tell you right now, Adam Quinn," Delores warned with a shaking finger in his direction. "If I don't like the look of this 'nanny' you hire, I'll show her the door."

Sienna buried a smile at the frustration splashed across Adam's features. He couldn't afford to offend his housekeeper, but he couldn't stand there and take orders, either. This baby had already thrown Adam's world out of balance and it was enthralling her to watch him find his feet and stand his ground.

"We'll deal with that if we have to," he said, and mollified Delores even without agreeing to her demands.

He was good. And, Sienna told herself, she should keep that in mind. Adam was fast, smart and unwavering when he wanted something. Why did she like that about him?

"Did Kevin send the things for the baby?"

Delores's lips twisted as if she were considering continuing the argument, but then she thought better of it and blew out a breath. "He did. There've been delivery trucks in and out of here all afternoon."

"Good. Where'd you set up the nursery?"

"Right where you told me to," she said. "The guest suite across from yours."

Sienna knew that room. It had once been Devon's whenever he was in town. Appropriate, she thought, that his son would sleep there now.

"Everything's in place?"

"It is." Delores walked to Sienna, threaded her arm through hers and led her to the staircase. "And Sienna, I've put you in the suite beside Adam's."

Oh boy. That might not be such a good idea. Being in the same house with Adam was going to be hard enough. Being in the bedroom right next door could be one temptation too many. Maybe she should just sleep on a couch in the baby's room. The minute that thought raced through her mind though, she was ashamed of herself for even considering using a baby to protect her from her own desires.

"Of course," Delores said, watching her, "if you'd rather a different room…"

"No." Damn her easy-to-read expressions. "No, it's fine. Thank you for taking care of it on such short notice."

"Oh, it's my pleasure. With just Adam in the house, I've little enough to do. It's nice having to scurry about occasionally." Together, they climbed the stairs with Delores talking a blue streak, the baby jumping up and down on her hip and Adam's silent footsteps right behind them.

Sienna could feel his presence and told herself that was not a good sign. She was going to have to be careful. To remember that she was only doing this for the sake of building her business. There was nothing personal between her and Adam and there wasn't going to be. Wanting him was one thing, having him would be something else altogether. That would be a complication she didn't need in her life. So she'd take care of the baby and keep to herself as much as possible. The best thing to do would be to find a good nanny. Fast.

Climbing the stairs to the second floor, Sienna focused on the house, the hall, the paintings on the walls, anything but the sensation of having Adam so close behind her. Cuddling the baby to her, she gently held his hand when he gave one of her earrings a hard tug and made a mental note to avoid dangling jewelry while she was here.

When Delores turned into a room on the left, Sienna followed her, and then stopped dead. For once in her life, she was stunned speechless. All she could do was walk to the center of the room and make a slow circle, taking it all in.

"All of this was done in one day?" The baby on her hip cooed as if in appreciation. And she couldn't blame him. It was the ideal nursery. Okay, yes, if given the opportunity, she would change the wall color from a boring soft gray to something a little more cheerful, but other than that, she was wildly impressed.

A cherrywood crib stood along one wall, all made up and ready for the baby, complete with a teddy bear in one corner. There were two dressers, an overstuffed rocking chair near one of the windows, low shelves holding a few books and toys, and a colorful rug covering the hardwood floor.

"I told him I wanted it ready by this afternoon," Adam said, giving the room a careful, thorough look.

"So naturally, it is." Sienna shook her head. She wasn't sure whether to be bemused or appalled. The man could order up something like this and not be surprised in the slightest when it was all just as he'd commanded.

"Problem?" he asked.

"No, of course not." Annoyance bubbled inside her and even Sienna couldn't have said exactly why. "You make demands and the world jumps."

One eyebrow lifted. "Not the world. Just the people who work for me."

Which now included her. At least temporarily. So she gave him a not so gentle reminder. "I don't jump."

One eyebrow lifted and his eyes narrowed on her. If that was the look he gave to recalcitrant employees, Sienna could see why they would hurry to do his bidding. But she wasn't so easily intimidated. She didn't need Adam Quinn's job for her livelihood. And it would save them both a lot of time if he got used to her defying him right from the beginning.

"I didn't ask you to jump," he pointed out.

"You might. I'm just letting you know beforehand that it's not going to happen."

"I'll make a note," he ground out.

"All right," Delores said, looking from one of them to the other. "I'll just take the baby downstairs and feed him while you two settle…whatever it is that needs settling." She plucked the baby from Sienna's hip. She didn't give either one of them another look before slipping out the door.

"I don't want to fight about this," she started saying.

"But you're going to anyway."

Sienna blew out a breath and shook her head. "Adam, you're entirely too used to people leaping into action whenever you speak."

"Is that right?" He folded his arms across his chest and stared down at her as if she were a fascinating bug under a microscope. Great.

"When was the last time someone told you no?"

"You mean besides you?" One eyebrow lifted.

"Yes, besides me." She wandered the baby's room, snatched the teddy bear from the crib and held it in both hands as she studied its ridiculously happy face.

"People argue with me all the time," he said.

She glanced at him. "Do they ever win?"

He didn't say anything to that and she knew she had him.

"So, no."

"And you know that, how?"

Her gaze snapped up to his. "Because it's who you are, Adam."

"Got me all figured out, do you?"

"Oh please," she said, dropping the bear back into the crib. "Don't look so offended. You know I'm right. But here's something you don't know." She lifted her chin defiantly. "Try to order me around and I'll leave."

A tight half smile curved his mouth briefly. "No you won't, Sienna." He reached up and loosened the knot of his tie, undid the top button of his shirt.

Just that simple action made him less formidable and even more attractive. Why was that open collar so sexy? Her stomach swirled with nerves that she tried desperately to tamp down.

"I saw the look on your face when you held the baby," he said, amusement coloring his words.

Annoyed, she said, "Stop reading my mind."

"And even if you didn't already love Jack, you wouldn't leave because you don't quit," he added, staring into her eyes.

True. It wasn't just the baby who would keep her here. She'd made an agreement and, for Sienna, that was now nonnegotiable. In fact, the one and only time in her life that she'd given up was when she'd ended her marriage. And she still felt a pang of guilt for it. As if he'd heard that thought, he spoke up.

"Don't." Adam held her gaze. "You stayed with Devon far longer than any other woman would have."

"He was my husband."

"Yeah." He nodded, scrubbed one hand across his face and muttered, "And my brother, so I know what I'm talking about."

"This isn't about Devon," she said, interrupting whatever else he might have said. "This is about me. Being here. With you. Earlier, when I agreed to do this, you didn't give me a chance to lay down a few rules of my own."

He stuffed his hands into his pockets, tipped his head to one side and waited.

Looking at him was hard, because it tested her own will. He was just too gorgeous. Too crabby. Too everything. "I'll take care of the baby, but I won't do it alone."

He frowned. "What're you talking about?"

"You." When he still frowned, she went on. "Jack is your nephew. You're his guardian so you'd better get to know him."

"He's six months old."

"He won't be forever, and even with a nanny, he's going to need *you*."

Adam inhaled sharply and for the first time since she'd known him, he looked worried. Was there really something Adam Quinn wasn't supremely confident about?

"Believe it or not," he muttered, "I'd already worked that out on my own."

"Glad to hear it. He's a baby, Adam. He just wants to be held. Loved. You don't have to have all the answers right now."

"Maybe not, but I prefer having all the answers."

"Who wouldn't? But sometimes it just doesn't work out like that."

"Getting philosophical on me?" he asked.

"Hardly. Just settling a few things." As if to prove to him—and herself—that he wasn't getting to her, she walked across the room and stopped right in front of him. "I'll do my job, Adam. But I don't take orders. Not from you. Not from anyone."

Gazes locked, they stared at each other for several humming seconds as tension built between them. Every instinct Sienna had wanted her to speak up, to smooth things over. To somehow take the sting out of the challenge she'd just tossed at his feet, because she knew powerful men could never resist flaunting that power. But she held her tongue. Because she and Adam had to understand each other before this little experiment started.

She gritted her teeth to lock her jaw shut and didn't even speak when he moved in close enough that his scent flavored every breath she drew. Tipping her head back, she continued to hold his gaze, and after another second or two of taut silence, he started talking. "Everyone who works for me takes orders— one way or another. You're no different, Sienna."

"Yes," she assured him with a smile. "I really am. You came to me, Adam. You needed my help."

A muscle in his jaw twitched and his dark eyes suddenly went even darker. She almost felt sympathy for him because clearly he didn't like being reminded that he'd had a problem he couldn't solve himself.

"I'm here now and I'll do what we agreed on," she continued. "But don't think you can pull the King of the Universe thing with me."

In an instant, the darkness in his eyes lifted and his mouth curved slightly. She really hated what that simple facial expression did to the pit of her stomach. "King of the Universe," he mused. "I like it."

Laughing, she said, "Of course you do." As her laughter faded, her smile remained because the tension had been broken and because, damn it, she liked him. Bossy attitude or not.

"You've got a great smile."

"What?"

"You heard me," he said, and reached out to lift a long, wavy lock of her hair. "I like your hair, too."

Her breath caught. "Thank you?"

His gaze locked with hers, he asked, "You know the only thing I ever envied of Devon's?"

Her heart was hammering in her chest. "What?"

"You."

"Adam…" Sienna took a long, shaky breath and though she tried to look away from his eyes, she couldn't quite manage it. So she saw the spark of heat flash there. Saw his eyes narrow as he bent his head to hers. Someone must have hit a supernatural pause button. Because the world stopped. Everything went quiet.

Outside, beyond the wall of glass, the June sky roiled with gray clouds, and in the distance, fog lay thickly on the surface of the ocean. A sea wind sent the flowers on the balcony into a twisting dance and the vibrant colors looked like a kaleidoscope. Inside, though, the world was still.

She should say something. *Do* something.

Her mind shouted warnings that she paid no attention to. Sienna's insides jumped up and down in excitement. Then she did exactly what she shouldn't have. She leaned into him. When his mouth met hers, Sienna felt the reaction shaking in her bones.

Electric. That's what he was to her. Dazzling. Sensory overload. One touch and her skin sizzled. Her blood burned. Her mouth went dry; her heart hammered in her ears. Her chest felt tight as his mouth moved over hers in a kind of hunger she'd never known. It was as if he was fighting his own desire even while feeding it. She knew how that felt because she was caught in the same sensations.

Her mouth opened beneath his and their tongues tangled desperately. He let one hand slide down her body until he was cupping her core. Even through the denim of her jeans, she felt the heat of him, the insistence of him as he pressed and rubbed. Riding the thrill of the moment, the rush of sensations, Sienna rocked her hips, riding his hand, building on what he was doing to her.

Adam groaned and Sienna echoed the sound. Her hands snaked up to hold on to his shoulders, luxuriating in the strength of him. His hand pressed harder against her center and all she could think was that she wished her jeans were gone so she could feel his touch on her bare skin. She trembled, tore her mouth from his and struggled for air.

"You're killing me," he muttered as his clever, clever fingers undid the button and zipper of her jeans.

"I don't want to kill you," she whispered. "I just want you."

He actually growled, a low, harsh scrape of sound that sent shivers coursing through her body. In one part of her mind, Sienna couldn't believe this was happening, and yet, another part of her sighed in satisfaction.

Then he slipped his hand beneath the slim band of her panties and touched her. She was hot, slick and ready and the moment he touched her, Sienna felt a *pop* of release. Her body bucked, she trembled and sucked in air like a drowning woman coming up for the third time.

She looked into his eyes as she whimpered his name and rode out the last of the tremors claiming her. When it was over, he withdrew his hand, released her and took a long step back.

Sienna swayed unsteadily, and clumsily did up her jeans while she fought for air. Her mind was a blur of thoughts, emotions, and her body was struggling just to remain upright. It had been so long since she'd felt anything like that ripple of pleasure, it was hard to slow down her racing heart.

Adam stared at her and she watched as desire drained from his gaze. His eyes were shuttered. Blank slates. She couldn't read what he was thinking, feeling, and she hated that in the span of moments, he could distance himself from what had just happened. Was he simply trying to pretend nothing had happened here?

Well, she wasn't going to let him. She was shaken, but she didn't believe in lying to herself—or anyone else for that matter. Sienna preferred to face things head-on.

Her mouth still vibrating from the pressure of his, her body still humming, she asked, "Why?"

"Good question." He took a step back, shaking his head. "When I have an answer, I'll let you know."

Shaking her head, she swallowed hard. "Adam—"

"Don't start talking about it, Sienna, or we won't be stopping with some kissing and groping."

"What if I don't want to stop?" There it was. Out in the open. So much for maintaining control. But the simple truth was, now that she'd had his hands on her, she wanted his touch again.

"It doesn't change anything. I don't want to stop, either," he admitted through gritted teeth. "And that's a damn good reason why we should."

"That makes zero sense," she said, getting her breath back, steadying herself as she faced him.

"Damn it, Sienna." He pushed one hand through his hair and blew out a breath. "For once, try not to argue with me on something."

"So we're just going to ignore what happened?"

"We're gonna try," he muttered, and grabbed up her duffel. "Meanwhile, I'll take your stuff to your room."

"Okay…" She waited until he started out the door to speak again and when she did, he stopped and turned his head to look at her. "But what if we can't ignore it, Adam?"

His gaze burned into hers for what felt like forever and the taut silence between them practically screamed. "Then I guess we'll have to find out what happens next."

He left and she stared at the empty space where

he'd been as if she could find answers to what she was feeling. Thinking. She hadn't counted on the desire she'd felt for him to be so easily stoked into an inferno. But now that it had been, she didn't want to deny it, either.

Since Devon's death, Sienna had been alone. By design. She'd concentrated on her business, on rebuilding her life. There'd been no time for men, even if she'd been interested, which she really hadn't been.

But now there was Adam.

And her emotions were so all over the place she couldn't pin a single one down long enough to examine it. She wasn't here to play house, though. To give in to the need for him that had always been there, just beneath the surface. And she'd do well to remember that.

When she was steady enough, she followed Adam to the suite that would be hers and told herself that she was going to have to be very careful for the next couple of weeks. Moving in with Adam was going to be a test. Yes, she wanted the new photography studio. Yes, she loved babies and looked forward to taking care of Devon's son.

All of that said, though, there was Adam to be considered. He was both drawing her in and pushing her away in equal measure.

But his kiss, his touch, was going to haunt her.

Five

"It's taken care of, Mother." Adam carried his cell phone across the office and stopped in front of one of the wide windows. While his mother ranted through the speaker, he stared out at the sea. Usually, he could find calm there. Not, it seemed, today.

More surfers than usual, he thought idly, but then there was a storm out there somewhere, making the waves higher than normal. And, he told himself, there was clearly a different kind of storm brewing with his mother in Florida.

"How?" Donna Quinn demanded. "How is anything being taken care of? You can't expect me to believe *you're* caring for that baby."

Was that really so implausible? God knew he couldn't do much worse than his own parents had. He was already regretting calling Donna Quinn to let her know about her grandson's existence. But, she'd had a right to know that her favored son had become a father just before he died.

"I'm going to hire a nanny," he said, working hard to hold on to a temper that seemed to flare into life at just the sound of his mother's voice.

"Your housekeeper is unqualified," she told him flatly. "You need a proper nanny."

Both eyebrows rose as did the temper beginning to bubble in the pit of his stomach. "As I said, I'm going to hire a nanny."

The door behind him opened and he turned to wave Kevin into the room.

"And until then?" Her voice went higher, more demanding and he was regretting putting her on Speaker.

"I've got someone temporarily."

"Who?"

Kevin grimaced and Adam knew just what his friend meant. His mother wouldn't be happy if she knew it was Sienna caring for the baby. Donna Quinn still blamed Sienna for the divorce and even for Devon's death, insisting that if Sienna had stayed in the marriage, Devon wouldn't have been in that damn speedboat. His mother was irrational, but unmovable.

"Don't worry about it," he hedged. "It's handled."

"If I weren't so far away," she vowed, "I'd do it myself."

Kevin snorted and Adam frowned at him. Though, hell, that remark had been laughable. Donna wasn't exactly maternal. Oh, she hadn't run out on them, but she'd turned Adam and Devon over to a procession of au pairs as soon as she could.

"Kevin just came in—" Devon told her and watched with evil satisfaction as Kevin paled and waved both hands as he shook his head in blind panic. God, it was tempting to get rid of his mother by handing her off to Kevin. But if he did, the other man might quit just to get even.

"Well." Donna sniffed, and her voice went even cooler than usual. "You tell him for me that I've still not forgiven him for not inviting me to his wedding and—"

"I'll tell him," Adam interrupted. "I've got work, Mother."

"Fine. I want regular reports on Devon's child."

"His name is Jack."

She huffed. "After his father. Why would he do that?"

"I don't know," Adam said.

"Probably to irritate me," she said, because in Donna's world all things were about her.

Adam didn't have the time or the inclination to listen to his mother rail about how she'd suffered during her marriage and how Adam's father had crushed her girlish spirit. Since he'd lived through it, he knew damn well there'd been plenty of crushing on *both* sides.

"I'll keep you posted, Mother." He hung up then, before she could say another word.

Adam took a deep breath and deliberately loosened his grip on the cell phone before he could shatter it.

"I thought you were going to throw me to the wolf," Kevin said.

"Thought about it," Adam admitted with a shrug. "Hell, anything to get the wolf off me."

He scrubbed the back of his neck, trying to ease the tension, but it didn't work. Nothing did when he had to deal with his mother. They'd never been close—Donna had devoted whatever motherly interest she possessed to Devon. Just as well, since her constant plotting, planning and conniving had driven Devon crazy enough that when he married Sienna, the two of them had moved to Italy—partly to escape Donna.

"We probably should have just invited her to the wedding," Kevin mused.

"Oh hell no." Adam shook his head, walked back to his desk and dropped into the chair. "She'd have turned the whole thing into a circus."

Kevin shuddered. "Yeah, I guess. But I'll be hearing about it forever."

"The price we pay for sanity." Adam leaned back and closed his eyes. "At least she's in Florida."

"True. From what I heard, it sounds like she's already focusing on the baby. Substitute for Devon?"

"That's probably her plan." Adam opened his eyes and gave Kevin a hard look. "But that's not going to happen."

"Good luck stopping her."

Adam picked up a stray pen and tapped it furiously against the desk. "Oh, I'll stop her. I'm not a kid anymore. She doesn't make the rules. I do."

"Okay, good." Kevin nodded and leaned back in his chair. "So how'd your first night as a daddy go?"

Adam winced. "I'm his uncle not his father."

"Uh-huh. Technically. In practice, you're a brand-new father. Got cigars?"

"You're not as funny as you think you are." Adam frowned, sighed and admitted, "It was a nightmare. He cried for two hours straight. Sienna and I traded off walking him. Think I did twenty miles."

Of course, the hardest part of that had been being with Sienna and not touching her again. He'd had just a small taste of her, and that had fed his hunger until it was now gnawing on his bones. His soul.

He'd told Sienna they were going to ignore what had happened. So far, that wasn't working. At least, not for him.

Kevin groaned in sympathy. "Be sure to tell Nick that story, will you?"

"Happy to." Pushing Sienna from his mind, he

said, "The kid's got a good set of lungs on him anyway."

"Uh-huh. How'd it go with Sienna?"

Adam speared him with a look. "What's that mean?"

Kevin shrugged. "It means she's gorgeous and you've always had a thing for her."

Adam sat up straight, tossed the pen down and then picked it up again. "You know, some people go their whole lives without a know-it-all best friend."

"Poor souls." Kevin grinned. "Talk."

"It went fine."

Kevin snorted. "You're a master storyteller."

"I don't *share,* Kevin, and you damn well know it."

"I live in hope, though. Seriously, Adam, you're wound so tight, keeping everything so locked down that one of these days you're just going to snap."

"Thanks for the warning. I'll keep it in mind."

"Or you could just tell me what the hell's going on," Kevin said, eyes narrowed on him.

"What do you want from me?" Adam shook his head and avoided eye contact. "She's there to take care of Jack. That's it."

"Well," Kevin said slowly, "that's about the saddest thing I've ever heard."

Adam wasn't going to get into this with Kevin. Hell, he was trying very hard to not even *think* about Sienna—so far with no success. But talking about her wouldn't help the situation. Especially since

Adam knew damn well that Kevin would encourage him to seduce Sienna. To go after what he wanted and worry about the fallout later.

Well hell. He didn't *need* encouragement.

"I'm not looking for a woman, Kevin." And before the man could make a smart-ass remark, he added, "*Or* a man."

"Don't knock it till you've tried it."

Adam snorted. "Yeah, I tried marriage once. Remember?"

"That didn't count."

"Really?" Leave it to Kevin to rewrite his own rules when it suited him. "Why not?"

"Tricia wasn't exactly the settle-down type."

"Maybe she wasn't the problem."

Kevin narrowed his gaze on him. "Feeling all introspective? Lack of sleep getting to you?"

"No." But if his short-lived marriage had done anything, it had proven to Adam that he sucked at sharing. Tricia wasn't good at it either, so between the two of them, they'd created the marriage from purgatory. Hardly hell, since they were never together enough to make each other miserable. It had just been a slow slide into indifference and then oblivion.

He liked his life just fine now. Living on his own meant no one was counting on him. No one else's needs depended on Adam. He could go home, have a drink and get some work done in the peace and quiet.

Of course, he reminded himself, all of that had just changed dramatically. Quiet was going to be hard to find now that he had Jack to think of. He would do his best by his nephew—but that didn't change one very important thing. He wasn't a commitment kind of guy. He liked women fine as long as they came and went from his life without causing a ripple.

Then memories of that kiss, the feel of Sienna's body trembling in his arms as she reached a quiet climax, flooded his mind. The look in her eyes, her mouth parted, breath coming fast, quick. The slick heat of her body and the driving need he'd been forced to strangle before he could toss her onto the nearest bed and find what he wanted most.

A ripple. The thought was laughable.

Those stolen minutes with Sienna had proven to him that her presence in his life would be more like a tidal wave. A tsunami that would wipe out the world he'd created for himself. And even knowing that, he couldn't deny that his body was still hard, tight, painful.

Desire continued to pound inside him. He'd spent what was left of the night before lying awake, with his body aching for what he refused to give it. He wasn't going to start up something with his brother's ex because it couldn't go anywhere. And damned if he'd use Sienna as badly as his brother had.

All he had to do was make it through the next

couple of weeks without touching her again. And that meant he had to keep his mind from wandering to thoughts of her, too.

"Haven't we got some actual *work* to do?" he asked abruptly, desperate for something else to think about.

Kevin gave him a long, considering look. "That's actually why I came in here in the first place. The Davidson Group called about the project in San Diego. They want an in-house meeting."

"Good. Set it up." This was what he needed. To keep his mind so full of work it had no room to torment him with images of Sienna.

Adam's company was behind a luxury hotel going up in the place of a derelict building that had been left to rot. "Get the latest sketches from the architect. Tell them we want the finals ready to roll. Get the Davidson people in here tomorrow afternoon. I want to move on this."

"Right." Kevin stood up. "One of our crews are on-site now, clearing it. Mike Jonas says it should be ready for the new foundation by the end of the week."

"Good. Keep me posted. If they run into any trouble, I want to know about it." Adam grabbed a thick stack of files and opened the one on top.

"You will, but they won't." Kevin tapped his iPad, calling up one of the lists he lived for. "Oh. Tracy said to tell you she's got the bid from the landscape gardeners on the Long Beach project. Said it's too high, but she'll get them down lower."

"Okay, and call the Realtor in Santa Barbara about that property we put a bid on. I want to know what's taking so long."

"Got it." Kevin headed for the door.

"Wait a minute," Adam said, and Kevin stopped, turning to look back at him. "Did you arrange for a crew to take care of the repairs at Sienna's place?"

He'd told Kevin what he wanted done as soon as he got to the office that morning. Whatever happened between him and Sienna, damned if Adam was going to let her live in a place that looked so run-down. Naturally, Kevin had argued with him about it, insisting that Adam talk to Sienna before they did any work, but Adam wasn't interested in an argument. The woman had too much pride for her own good. So he'd just take the decision out of her hands. She'd be grateful. Eventually.

"I did," Kevin said reluctantly. He pulled up the schedule on his iPad. "Toby Garcia's going to take a few of the guys off the school building in Mission Viejo."

"Are we on schedule there?" Adam signed one of the letters Kevin had brought him and looked up at his friend.

"All on track. They're wrapping things up this week, so Toby felt safe pulling a few of the guys off that job." Kevin looked at him. "But I still think—"

"Yeah, I know what you think." Adam waved one hand at him dismissively. "I told you what I want. New roof, paint, any repairs, fix the damn cracks in her sidewalk, too," Adam muttered. "She's always staring into a camera lens so she'll kill herself on that walk sooner or later."

Kevin laughed. "Got it."

"And the garage door." Adam tossed his pen aside. "It looks like it's original to the house and that puts it around the forties. I want an automatic door installed so she can park that crappy car of hers inside without having to get out and try to wrestle the door into submission."

Still laughing and shaking his head, Kevin made more notes. "And since we're not talking to the owner of the house, what color would you like for the new paint?"

"Had to get a shot in?" Adam asked wryly.

"Just a reminder that you're asking for trouble doing this without talking to her first."

"Thanks. Look. I could have asked her, but she'd have said no, so why bother?" Adam grabbed his pen and signed another letter after scanning it quickly. "Go with blue. Soft, not bright. White trim. Paint the damn porch, too. Looks terrible."

"Adam, I say again, she's going to be pissed."

"She can be as mad as she wants to be. The house will still be fixed."

Kevin's eyebrows went sky-high and he shook his head. "Better you have to face her with this than me."

Adam snorted. "Stop worrying. She'll love it so much she'll get over the mad fast enough." And if she didn't, Adam knew that he'd at least enjoy the argument. That woman had a head like a rock, but eventually, she'd be grateful he swooped in and fixed her house. Now all he had to do was replace that car.

"Right." Kevin nodded. "Please let me be there when you tell her what we did. I'd love to see how fast she gets over the mad."

Adam scowled at him. "Think you know her better than I do?"

"I think you just ride in and take over."

Hard to argue with that.

"And," Kevin continued, "I know I'd be furious if you just *decided* on your own to redo my house without asking."

"Then I won't do your house."

Kevin shrugged. "It's your neck. Anyway, once Toby's done at Sienna's, he'll head the crew doing the church job in Lake Forest."

"That'll work," Adam said, pleased at the change in subject. "We've got a meeting in Santa Barbara next week, right?"

"Yeah, with the group looking to fund a new golf course."

Adam smiled and leaned back. "How's the design coming?"

"The team's working on it, but they hit a snag."
Kevin waved his hand. "Something about a par three
overlooking the ocean but needing more room for the
bunkers they want to add."

"Send me the specs. I'll take a look at home tonight."

"Already sent them to your email."

"Great. Thanks."

Kevin turned to leave, but Adam stopped him.
"I'll be bringing Jack in tomorrow. I'm going to need
help with him."

"Yeah," Kevin said, laughing as he closed the office door. "You really will."

Sienna took dozens of pictures.

Little Jack Quinn was the perfect subject. Of
course, even if the adorable baby hadn't been there,
Sienna would have had plenty of targets for her lens.
The house. The grounds. The views. On the second-
floor balcony, surrounded by terra-cotta pots filled
with flowers that spilled over onto glass-topped
tables, she shot so many images, she'd be sorting
through them for hours.

And Jack was there, at her feet, laughing, bouncing in a walker that contained far too many bells and
other assorted noisemakers. Once Delores left for
her vacation, it had been just Sienna and Jack in the
big house. And after a couple of hours alone with a
baby, Sienna had a whole new respect for mothers.

"Who knew you could be so demanding?" she

asked, smiling and talking in a singsong tone that
made the tiny boy laugh in response.

Instantly, she felt a flutter around her heart and
told herself that Adam wasn't the only danger in the
Quinn household. She could easily fall in love with
this baby. Which wasn't a good idea, since the moment Adam hired a nanny, Jack would no longer be
a part of her life.

"But I'm going to love you anyway, aren't I?"

He giggled, slapped both arms against the walker
and kicked his chubby little legs. She took another
quick shot and admired it on the view screen. "You
just don't take a bad picture, do you? Sort of like
your father. And your uncle."

She sat back into the deep cushions of the couch
and watched Jack push off on his tiny feet and roll
along the floor of the great room. Watery sunlight
slipped through the gray clouds to lay what seemed
like a mystical glow on the scene. The house was
quiet but for the baby's gurgles, laughs and slaps.
She lifted her ever-present camera and took a few
shots of the tiny boy with the magnificence of the
house surrounding him. As she looked at her view
screen, Sienna thought about what it would be like
for him, growing up here with Adam.

Would the baby find the father he needed? Would
Adam turn Jack's care completely over to a nanny?
She frowned at the thought, then reminded herself
that Adam had been right there with her the night

before when they couldn't get Jack to sleep. They'd taken turns walking through the house, murmuring and consoling the baby who had to have been confused at his new surroundings. Adam had been patient and kind, and being that close to him in the stillness of the night had made her feel too much.

Of course, he'd been even closer yesterday afternoon. With his hands on her. His mouth on hers. Sienna trembled, remembering those few stolen moments when she'd shattered in his arms. A swift jolt of heat swamped her and sent flames licking along her bloodstream. She wanted to feel it all again. Feel *more.* For years, Sienna had tried to ignore what Adam made her want. Need. Now it was as if her body and mind had been unleashed and she wanted to revel in it.

This was so not good.

Before she could get any further on that train of thought, her cell phone rang and Sienna grabbed at it like a lifeline. "Cheryl, hi."

Best friend, mother of three and the voice of sanity when Sienna needed it.

"Hi back. Weren't we supposed to have lunch over here today?"

"Oh God." Face palm. She sat back and let her head drop against the dark brown leather couch. Jack paused in his play to give her a quizzical look. She smiled at him as she said, "I completely forgot. I'm so sorry."

Cheryl laughed. "Hey, no problem. Just glad to know it's not *my* mind dissolving."

"No, it's totally me." Sienna watched the baby roll over across the floor, slapping both hands onto the bells attached to the walker tray. "Something came up yesterday and—"

"And apparently is still going on today?" Cheryl interrupted. "Intriguing."

Intriguing. Well, that was one word for it. Another was *crazy.* Or *masochistic.* Or, given enough time, she could no doubt come up with plenty of words to describe what was going on right now. Sienna sighed. "You're not going to believe this, but I'm at Adam's house."

There was a long pause. "Adam? As in Adam your ex-brother-in-law? Adam Sex-on-a-Stick Quinn?"

In spite of everything, Sienna laughed. "He's not on a stick."

"Maybe not," Cheryl mused, "but I'm betting he's got a '*big* stick.'"

Instantly, her mind conjured up images of Adam, naked, and everything in Sienna curled up and whimpered. "Really? You're not helping."

"Disagree," her friend countered. "You've been telling me about Adam for two years. Do you really think I haven't done a little imagining from time to time? For example, my Charlie has a terrific stick."

Sienna laughed. "I do *not* need to know that."

"How can I make my friends jealous if I don't brag?"

Shaking her head, Sienna rolled her eyes and asked, "Does Charlie know how often you brag?"

"Why do you think he loves me so much?" Cheryl paused and asked, "But enough about my love life—what're you doing at Adam's house?"

"It's a long story." And it felt as if she'd been involved in this story for a lot longer than just a couple of days. But then, she'd first met Adam, first felt that quick zip of attraction for him, almost four years ago. So was it any wonder that as soon as they were really alone together, it was almost as if they always *had* been?

"I've got a hot cup of tea and the kids are outside playing. I have the time, so if it's a long story, then you'd better get started."

So Sienna launched into an explanation, and the more she talked, the more improbable it all sounded, even to her. Adam had appeared in her life, turned it upside down and here she was, still trying to make sense of it all.

Then she looked at baby Jack and smiled as he slapped at the tray of toys with two chubby fists. "Bottom line, I'm staying with Adam until he hires the right nanny."

"Wow." Cheryl took a breath and sighed it out again. "It's a soap opera. You're even living in that mansion you drove me past one time."

"I am, and it's still more impressive inside than out," Sienna said, glancing round the great room, admiring the soft warmth of the place with the view of the cold ocean beyond the glass. A sea wind tossed the flowers on the balcony into a riot of colors and the thick gray clouds scuttled back and forth across the sky like prizefighters waiting for their chance to enter the ring.

"It's amazing. You, a baby and the Lord of the Manor. I was wrong. It's not a soap opera. It's a gothic novel." Cheryl warned, "Whatever you do, stay out of the attic. That's where the hero stores his crazy wife."

Laughing, Sienna said, "Sorry to disappoint, but there is no attic. There is however, a terrific view of the ocean from almost every room."

"Well, that's just mean," Cheryl said, a whine evident in her tone. "While you're there, I have to come over and see it."

"Absolutely. I'd love the company. When I'm not working, it's just Jack and I here in the house." Sienna grinned at the baby, bouncing up and down on his toes. "He's adorable, but not much for conversation."

"You think that's a bad thing," Cheryl said on a chuckle. "Then they start talking. So when do you work next?"

"Tomorrow I've got two shoots, back-to-back at Huntington Central Park." She still had to get her equipment together and ready, but there was time.

"What'll you do with the baby?"

Smiling, Sienna said, "Tomorrow, he's all Adam's."

Cheryl laughed. "I'd actually pay to see that."

"Me, too." Sienna took a breath and smiled at the thought. "But can you come over the following day?"

"You bet. I'll take the kids to their grandmother's."

"You don't have to," Sienna assured her. Cheryl's kids were great and she was sure Jack would enjoy them.

"Trust me—it's a win-win. I'll have a couple of hours to myself and my mother-in-law will be happy with me for a change."

"Okay, I'll have wine and snacks."

"You don't have to sell me," Cheryl said on a laugh, "but good to know."

When she hung up, Sienna looked down at the little boy who had managed to scoot across the room and right up to her. He grinned and a long line of drool slid from his open mouth. His eyes were shining and when he squealed in delight, Sienna smiled. He was already burrowing his way into her heart, and she knew that when she left she would miss little Jack desperately.

But she had a feeling that leaving Adam was going to be the hardest thing she'd ever done.

Six

A few hours later, Adam walked in the door to find Sienna in the great room and no sign of the baby. He took the moment before she noticed him to look her over, top to toe. Hunger stirred inside him in a wave that was so high, so powerful, it was all he could do to control the urge to grab her and indulge himself with the heady taste of her again.

She was curled up in a big chair, long blond hair hanging over her left shoulder and across the top of her breasts. Her legs were tucked up beneath her and she had her head propped on one fist as she flipped through an open magazine on her lap. For a second or two, he wondered why it was *she* who drove him crazy.

She wasn't trying to be seductive. She was dressed simply and was totally unaware of his presence—and yet, Sienna West tied him into knots that were only tightening by the hour. Taking a breath, he steadied himself and spoke up. "Baby wear you out in one day?"

She jolted a little in surprise, then her blue eyes shifted to him and locked on. "Turns out babies are *not* easy." Then she smiled teasingly. "But you'll find that out for yourself tomorrow."

"Yeah," he said, as an unfamiliar feeling he thought might be *cowardice* whipped through him. "About that."

Sienna gave him a stern look that did nothing to dissipate the desire he felt for her. "No way you're backing out, Adam. We have a deal."

He met her determined gaze for a long moment before nodding. "You're right. We do." He shrugged out of his suit jacket and loosened his tie and collar button. Tossing the jacket onto the nearest chair, he plopped down in another one. "I'll take him with me to work tomorrow."

Sienna grinned and he really hated that his body fisted in reaction, but there didn't seem to be anything he could do about it. "I'd love to see you dealing with the baby during some high-powered meeting."

"You think I can't?" Even though he'd thought the same himself only seconds ago, he brushed aside her disbelief. "I absolutely could, but I don't have to. When I'm in a meeting, Kevin will take care of him." In fact, he was looking forward to the expression on his friend's face when Adam handed Jack over to him.

She tipped her head to one side and watched Adam with a slight smile curving her mouth. "He might quit."

"Not a chance," he said, shaking his head. "He'll complain, but he'll do it."

Adam thought about getting a beer from the wet bar across the room, but it seemed like too much trouble. Then she spoke, and he had to wonder if Sienna was reading *his* mind for a change.

"Want a beer?"

He frowned. "You don't have to wait on me, Sienna."

"Oh, if I *had* to," she assured him, "I wouldn't."

He grinned briefly. "In that case, yeah. I would like a beer."

She unfolded from the chair and he watched her walk barefoot across the room, admiring the view. Her jeans were worn and faded and hugged her legs like long-lost lovers coming together. The tail of her pale blue dress shirt hung past her butt and he was disappointed that particular view was hidden. She bent to the bar refrigerator and came out with two cold bottles. She delivered one to him and kept the other, twisting off the top and taking a drink.

"Long day?" he asked, sipping at his own beer.

"You could say so." She studied the label on the

green bottle, then looked at him again. "Jack's a sweetheart, but he needs constant attention. It's exhausting. I don't know how parents do it."

"Some don't," he muttered, and was surprised when she picked up on it.

"Yes," she said softly. "Devon told me a little about your folks."

Adam chuckled and lifted his beer in salute. "Oh, I'm sure he had plenty to say."

Shaking her head, she said, "Not really. Just that they were divorced and that your mom was a little... clingy."

"Nice word for it." Adam rested the bottle against his abdomen and studied her silently as he decided whether or not to say any more about it.

Then he realized there was no one to protect— Devon was gone, so was their father and as for Adam's mother, no woman had needed protection less. Besides, Sienna had obviously been told some of it already, so why bother pretending the Quinn family was anything but dysfunctional?

"Devon was the golden child," he said on a sigh. "Our mother really wasn't a hands-on parent when we were little. She was too busy with clubs and charity and society. But once Devon hit twelve or so, she started hanging on his every word." He frowned, remembering. "Maybe it was because Dad started cheating on her about that time. Maybe she wanted

Devon to love only her. I don't know. She probably doesn't, either.

"Anyway, if that was her plan, it didn't work. She lavished attention on him until all Devon could think about was getting away."

Sienna picked at the label on her beer bottle with her fingernail. "He did say that your dad was easier to deal with…"

Adam laughed shortly when he glanced at her again. "He was. Because Dad didn't really give a damn what we did as long as our jobs got done."

Gritting his teeth, he clammed up, rethinking the decision to talk about the past. What the hell? He never told anyone about his parents. Even Kevin only knew bits and pieces of it and only because he'd actually seen some of it for himself when he'd gone home with Adam during college vacations.

What was the point of rehashing the past? It was useless and served nothing. When Sienna spoke, she broke his train of thought and he was ridiculously grateful.

"So does your mom know about Jack?"

"She does now." Remembering that phone call earlier, he took another sip of beer. Giving a snort of derisive laughter, he added, "She's so worried she's going to stay right where she is."

Sienna laughed a little, too. "Sorry. But in her defense, it's a lot to take in and she did just lose her son."

He looked at her and noticed that she was silhouett

now against the wall of windows behind her. Streaks of pink and gold and deep red shot through the clouds as the sun began to set and her eyes shone in the shadows. Her features were again easy to read and he saw sympathy for his mother written there. He couldn't really say why that annoyed him.

"You don't have to defend her," Adam said. "Or feel sorry for her. She's not coming, and it's better for all of us that she's not."

Sienna bit down on her bottom lip. "Does your mother know I'm the one watching Jack for you?"

The question came soft and low. So low he almost missed it. "No," he said, taking another sip of his beer. "I didn't see the point in stirring her up."

Sienna sighed and set her beer on the table in front of her. "She still blames me."

Adam shrugged that off, sat forward and braced his forearms on his thighs. Meeting her gaze squarely, he said, "If she does, that's her deal, Sienna. Nothing you should even think about. She has to blame someone—God knows she'd never blame herself for Devon's problems—so you're handy."

Sienna smiled sadly and shook her hair back from her face. "Or, maybe she's a little right."

"No. She's not." He wouldn't let Sienna accept his mother's implied accusations as if they were deserved. Donna Quinn had always been unreasonable when it came to Devon. She'd seen only what she had wanted to see and disregarded the reality that didn't quite measure up.

Sienna tipped her head to one side and her hair fell like a golden waterfall. He'd spent most of the day with her face, her voice, her scent, haunting him. He never should have kissed her, and he knew it because now all he could think of was tasting her again.

"You sound sure," she said.

"I am. Hell, Sienna, you stayed with Devon two years. That's a damn record." He pushed to his feet, because he couldn't remain so close to her without reaching out to touch her. And if he touched her, he wouldn't stop. Riding the energy pulsing inside him, Adam walked to the bar, set the beer down and turned back to look at her from across the room. It was safer, keeping a distance between them.

Too bad this wasn't far enough.

He took a deep breath, grateful that her scent wasn't filling his lungs. Didn't know if he could take that just now. "Don't get me wrong. I loved my brother but that didn't make me blind to who he was."

She frowned slightly. "He wasn't a bad guy."

Adam rubbed one hand across his eyes as if he could wipe away the memories suddenly flooding his mind. "Oh, I know that. But he wasn't a *good* guy, either."

She didn't comment on that and Adam almost congratulated her on her restraint. Yeah, she'd been married to the man, but Adam had grown up with

Dear Reader,

IT'S A FACT: if you answer 4 quick questions, we'll send you **4 FREE REWARDS!**

I'm not kidding you. As a leading publisher of women's fiction, we value your opinions… and your time. That's why we are prepared to **reward** you handsomely for completing our mini-survey. In fact, we have 4 Free Rewards for you, including 2 free books and 2 free gifts.

As you may have guessed, that's why our mini-survey is called **"4 for 4"**. Answer 4 questions and get 4 Free Rewards. It's that simple!

Thank you for participating in our survey,

Pam Powers

To get your 4 FREE REWARDS:
Complete the survey below and return the insert today to receive 2 FREE BOOKS and 2 FREE GIFTS guaranteed!

"4 for 4" MINI-SURVEY

1 Is reading one of your favorite hobbies?
☐ YES   ☐ NO

2 Do you prefer to read instead of watch TV?
☐ YES   ☐ NO

3 Do you read newspapers and magazines?
☐ YES   ☐ NO

4 Do you enjoy trying new book series with FREE BOOKS?
☐ YES   ☐ NO

YES! I have completed the above Mini-Survey. Please send me my 4 FREE REWARDS (worth over $20 retail). I understand that I am under no obligation to buy anything, as explained on the back of this card.

225/326 HDL GMYG

FIRST NAME

LAST NAME

ADDRESS

APT.#

CITY

STATE/PROV.

ZIP/POSTAL CODE

READER SERVICE—Here's how it works:

Devon. Had known him better than anyone else possibly could. And he still felt a tug of shame for how Devon had lived his life.

Adam believed that a man was only as good as his word. In that respect alone, Devon had been a disappointment. The man constantly made promises that weren't kept because something more interesting came up. It wasn't that Devon went out of his way to be a dick. It came naturally to him. But his smile, his charm had always been there to dig him out of whatever hole he found himself in.

"I don't know what you want me to say, Adam."

"Not a damn thing. You don't have to explain my brother to me or why you finally left him." He sighed and shook his head. Devon was gone and there was nothing to be gained by wishing things had been different. "But you don't have to pretend you were happy with Devon, either."

She laughed a little, but there was a tinge of sadness in the sound, too. "No point in that, really. If I'd been happy I wouldn't have divorced him."

"Well yeah, that's true enough." He looked at her as she stood up and walked toward him. Adam stiffened and hoped to hell she didn't come too close. Those eyes of hers held his gaze and he couldn't have looked away if it had meant his life. As she came near, he said, "Devon cared about Devon. He was my brother and I loved him. But I watched him blow up every relationship he ever had. Before you and after you, he couldn't be happy with anyone else because *he* wasn't happy."

"He thought he was," Sienna said.

"No he didn't. Not really." Adam took a drink of the beer he didn't want anymore. "He just kept himself so busy—yachts, jets, parties—that he didn't have time to sit down and realize that his life was so damn empty, every breath he took echoed."

"He did what he liked doing, Adam."

"Mostly," he acknowledged. "But he lost something when he left the business. Hell, I think he lost himself. He thought it'd be easier, being away from the family. From expectations. Not his fault entirely. Our dad was hard on both of us," he mused. "But he rode Devon all the time. Maybe because our mom went hard the other way."

Over the years, Adam had seen Devon change in response to his position in the family. To their father, Devon was the errant boy. The screwup. The guy who never got anything right. To their mother, he was the golden child who should be coddled and adored.

Devon became the bone that two dogs were fighting over. And Adam was on the outside, looking in. He couldn't change his parents, couldn't reach his brother, so he'd channeled everything he had into building his business. And when his father died, he'd merged the two companies. He'd bought Devon out when it became all too clear that his little brother was only interested in indulging himself and that his lifestyle was starting to affect the business.

"I let him go," Adam admitted, though the confession stung, even so long after.

"What do you mean?"

He looked into her eyes and for the first time, he couldn't read what she was thinking. Was that because he didn't want to know? Didn't want to see her blame him for what had become of Devon?

He set his beer onto the wet bar, then stuffed his hands into his pockets. "Devon wanted out. Wanted to get away from our mother, out from under the company and I let him go. Instead of kicking his ass, making him see that he should stay, work through whatever the hell was bugging him—I bought him out because he was driving me batshit. And I watched him leave. Never tried to stop him."

Sienna moved to the bar and leaned both arms on the cool, sleek polished top. "It was his decision."

"Was it?" Adam shook his head, then pushed one hand through his hair, irritated with himself. With Devon. With the whole damn situation. "I don't know. By the time he left, he was rarely at the office anyway, but if I'd said something, maybe he'd have straightened up. No way to know."

"He couldn't stay, Adam. You couldn't have changed his mind." She walked behind the bar and opened the fridge.

Adam spoke up quickly. "No thanks. I don't want another beer. Hell, I don't want this one."

"Me, either," she said, and stood up, handed him a bottle of water instead.

Ruefully, he smiled. He should have known she wouldn't do what he expected. "Thanks."

Opening her own bottle, she said, "Y'know, Devon told me about how much fun the two of you had when you started your business."

Surprised, but pleased, Adam said, "He did?"

"He missed those days, I think." She took a sip of water. "He missed *you*. But your mom drove him crazy, though he never said much about your father."

"Not shocking," Adam told her, and took a drink to ease his suddenly dry throat. "Dad and Devon never got along."

"He wouldn't have stayed, Adam," she said again, her tone practically demanding that he believe her. "He wanted to get away and you couldn't have changed his mind."

"Yeah, probably not." At least, he hoped not. Adam hated to think that when his brother had needed him most, Adam had taken the easy route and given Devon exactly what he wanted—instead of what he needed.

Frowning, he took another drink of water and watched the woman standing too close to him. He'd never talked about any of this before. Not even to

Kevin. Adam had hung on to the tattered threads of his own guilt about Devon for years.

Because his father hadn't resented him and his mother had mostly ignored him, Adam hadn't had the same problems his younger brother had had. It wasn't his fault, Adam knew, but that knowledge didn't stop the guilt that crept up and slapped at him when he least expected it. Still, Devon was gone now and the best Adam could do for his little brother was to make sure Devon's son was happier than his father had been.

Thinking of Jack, Adam changed the subject abruptly. "I didn't even ask you about the baby. Where is he?"

She smiled and Adam tried to ignore the burn he felt in response.

"He's sleeping. I've got the baby monitor over there on the coffee table so I can hear him."

"Right. Of course." He capped off the water bottle. "Well, him sleeping's a good sign. Maybe he won't be up all night again."

"I think he'll be okay," she said. "He was probably just scared of a new place and new people."

"Hope you're right," he muttered. "How'd the first day with him go? Any problems?"

"No," she said with another smile.

"So, any tips for tomorrow?"

"You bet. Don't take your eyes off of him for a second." She shook her head and gave a little laugh.

"He can't even walk yet, but put him on the floor and he's scooting and crawling a million miles per hour. And in his walker? Forget it. He figured out really fast how to make that little sucker move like a race car."

"Great..."

"And he's really picky about his food," she mused. "We went through a couple different kinds of baby food with him spitting most of it out. Thankfully, my friend Cheryl suggested banana slices. Those, he chowed down."

This was all so far out of his experience, Adam had a momentary pang. He was responsible for a tiny human. It would be up to him to make sure Jack was always secure. Safe. How would he be able to find a nanny in the next two weeks who he could trust enough with Jack's safety? How did parents do this?

"Oh, and he tried to pull himself up and bonked his forehead on the coffee table."

"He hit his head?" Adam blurted out as a quick jolt of what felt like *fear* scrambled through his veins. Before this baby entered his life, Adam had never been afraid of a damn thing.

"He's fine, Adam," Sienna said. "He didn't even cry, really. Just rubbed his forehead and looked surprised. As if the coffee table had betrayed him or something."

"Okay." He relaxed a little and scrubbed one hand across the back of his neck. "Who the hell can I trust with him?" he asked as his new reality came crashing down on him. "Basically, I have to find a nanny who's a world-class sprinter, a paramedic and a chef."

Sienna laughed and shook her head. "Don't make it all sound so impossible. People have been raising children for thousands of years."

"I haven't," he reminded her. Taking a long swig of water to ease the knot in his throat, he muttered, "I never wanted kids, you know."

"Like Devon, then."

He looked at her. "Yeah. Can't really blame either of us. We were raised by wolves. What the hell did we know about how to treat a kid?"

"Easy," Sienna replied, and reached out to lay her hand on top of his. "Just do everything your own parents *didn't* do. You know what you wanted from them when you were young. Give Jack what you needed and didn't get."

Sounded reasonable. And yet, there was still a slender thread of fear spooling inside him. It was a huge obligation and he didn't want to screw it up. *So, don't.* Even as those words echoed in his mind, he reminded himself that he'd never failed once when he went after something. If Jack was his goal, then he'd do it right. Adam didn't accept failure.

He looked at Sienna's much smaller hand on his and concentrated on the heat passing back and forth between them. Lifting his gaze to hers, he saw a flash of understanding in those blue eyes just before she pulled her hand back.

"You're a smart guy, Adam," she said blithely. "You'll figure it out. Now how about dinner?"

He accepted the change of subject, the coolness in her eyes because damned if it didn't make things easier. Right now, easy sounded pretty good. "You *cooked*?"

"No, I dialed." She shook her hair back from her face. "I found a nearby Chinese restaurant and called. Turns out you have an account there."

Adam smiled. "When Delores isn't here, it's better I don't try to cook."

"No breakfast in bed for me then, huh?" She grinned. "I'll keep that in mind."

His eyes narrowed on her and he picked up her hand, rubbing his thumb across her knuckles. "When I get you into bed, trust me when I say you won't be thinking about food."

Adam had the satisfaction of seeing heat burst in her eyes like fireworks. Then she pulled her hand free again. "Well right now, I'm hungry."

"Me, too," he assured her.

"For food," she said.

"That, too," he murmured. Until just that moment, they'd both been ignoring the damn elephant in the room. Time to notice it. "You avoided me this morning."

She pressed her lips together. "I evaded. That's different."

"No, it's not."

"Okay, you're right." She crossed her arms over her chest in an unmistakable, self-defensive posture. "I wasn't ready to talk to you about what happened. So I hid out with the baby. How pitiful is that?"

"I did the same thing," Adam admitted with a shrug. "Hell, I left the house without coffee. Trust me when I say, that's pitiful. Avoiding you didn't work. though. I still thought about you today."

"Did you?"

How could he not? he wondered silently. Hell, just look at her. Blond, blue eyes, long legs, full breasts and a smile that curved her delicious mouth into tempting lines. "I don't want to think about you, Sienna."

She took a deep breath and he couldn't help but notice the rise and fall of the breasts he wanted his hands on.

"I don't want to think about you, either," she admitted.

"Well then, seems we have a problem."

"Probably," she agreed. "But we can worry about that *after* we eat, right?"

Before, during, after... But all he said was, "Yeah, we can do that."

"Come on, Gypsy. Don't make us look bad in front of all those snooty cars."

The next morning, Sienna glanced at Adam's fleet of vehicles with a touch of envy mixed with exasperation. How did one man need six cars? The garage and carport area behind the house was enormous. He'd moved his Land Rover out of the garage to make room for her car and she had to admit that alongside the sleek, waxed and gleaming autos, Gypsy looked a little worn.

"But looks don't matter," Sienna soothed as she patted the dashboard. "You're just as good as those other cars. Now, come on. Show them all. Be a good girl." She tried turning the key again and got exactly nothing. Not even an engine cough. As if her car wasn't even *trying* to start.

Defeated, Sienna slumped in the seat, and then jolted when Adam leaned down and asked, "Problem?"

She gave him a sneer. He was probably enjoying this. Nothing the man liked better than being right. "Gypsy won't start."

"Imagine that." He straightened up and jostled baby Jack into a more comfortable position on his shoulder.

Things had been tense between them since last night. They'd retired to their separate bedrooms and Sienna had spent most of the night lying awake, wondering if he was regretting the decision to *not* have sex as much as she was.

But there were a lot of good reasons.

First, Devon, naturally. And, did they really know each other well enough to take that step? Sienna wasn't a one-night-stand kind of girl. Never had been. Yet, if she slept with Adam, she had to admit to herself that it would just be a fleeting thing. The man hadn't made a secret of the fact that he hated the very idea of commitment. So there was a lot to consider that was absolutely no consolation at all, when what she wanted was to jump into his bed and enjoy herself.

Looking down at her, he asked, "So. Is this the kind of 'adventure' you like, or would you rather drive one of my cars to your appointment?"

Oh, she wished she could refuse the offer, but if she didn't leave in the next few minutes, she'd be late. Swallowing her pride with a good dose of irritation, she said, "Thanks. I'd appreciate it."

He waved his free arm toward the cars waiting in the spotless white and stainless steel garage. "Take your pick. The keys are in a cabinet on the far wall."

Said the king to the peasant. Rolling her eyes, she climbed out, retrieved her camera bag and then muttered, "Thanks."

"I'm sorry, what?"

She shot him a look, then reluctantly smiled at the glint of amusement in his eyes. "Fine. Thank you. You were right, oh, King of the Universe. My car needs work."

He snorted. "Your car needs a burial."

Jack laughed and slapped Adam's cheek. He caught the baby's hand in his and held on. Why did he look so damn sexy holding the tiny boy?

"I'd be insulted by that, but—" She looked at Gypsy and had to admit he had a point. Her car had definitely seen better days. Gypsy was really old and she'd lived a hard life. It was time to find a new used car. "I'll take your Explorer if that's okay."

"Fine. I've got his car seat set up in the Rover." Adam looked at the baby as he would an alien being.

He was way out of his depth and yet, Adam wasn't trying to evade the new responsibility dumped on him. She admired him for that. Heck, there was a lot she admired about him. This wouldn't be easy, incorporating a child into his life, but Adam was already making concessions. As she watched, Jack gave Adam a wide, toothless smile and just for an instant, Adam smiled back. Then he glanced down at his suit jacket. "Drool. Perfect."

She laughed. "Okay, really I have to go. You want me to stop at the office to pick him up when I'm finished?"

Adam's whole face lit up. "You do that and I'll buy you a *car*."

Laughing again, Sienna started toward the Explorer. "Not necessary. Dinner would be good, though."

Seven

Jack became the office mascot.

Adam ran his meeting, settled a few things with the Davidson Group, wound things up with Kevin, who'd also been in the meeting while Tracy in accounting watched Jack, and then Adam had to hunt down his nephew. Apparently, tiny Jack Quinn was now the star of Quinn Development Enterprises.

First, he went to Tracy, who was supposed to look after Jack during the meeting. But when one of their top clients dropped by, she'd handed Jack off to Kara. Then Kara was needed to research one of the new projects, so Tom in IT took over. Like Kara, Tom had kids of his own, so one small baby was no problem. But then a computer crashed and Tom handed Jack off to Nancy at reception and by the time Adam finally caught up to the traveling baby, Jack was eating banana slices in the employee break room with Sienna.

"Not surprising," Adam murmured. "The kid's been all over the place…"

Standing in the doorway, Adam watched the baby squash bananas in his fists, and then laugh up at Sienna. She smiled at the little boy and everything inside Adam fisted. Her blond hair hung loose around her shoulders. Her blue eyes were shining. She wore a lemon yellow T-shirt that hugged her body, with a neckline that scooped low enough to give him a peek at the top of her breasts. Her jeans were faded and her sneakers were purple. He laughed to himself. Of course she would wear purple shoes.

A wild, barely controllable surge of pure lust rose up inside him, making breathing difficult and walking near impossible. Last night had been the longest of his life. Logically, he knew they'd done the right thing, pulling back from each other after dinner rather than giving in to what they both wanted. But logic didn't have a hell of a lot to do with what he was feeling right now.

"You're staring," she said, and slowly swiveled her head around to look at him.

"I like the view."

Her eyes flashed and he went so hot it was a wonder he didn't simply spontaneously combust. There she sat holding a laughing baby and all Adam could think about was tearing her clothes off and stretching her out on the break table. Damn it, he never should have touched her in the first place. Those few stolen moments, her quick breathing and soft sighs as her body trembled at his caresses had reawakened every damn instinct and urge he possessed.

Jack squealed in delight when he saw his uncle, then threw a slice of banana at him and Adam almost thanked the boy for shattering the tension in the room. Staring at Jack's round little face, with his wide-open mouth blasting a huge smile and his big eyes twinkling, Adam felt a surge of warmth he really hadn't expected. He'd never wanted children, yet here he was now, a surrogate father. And if he were being honest, he could admit at least to himself, that he hadn't been at all sure he was up to the task of giving the boy the kind of love he deserved. Yet now, love simmered warmly inside him and he could acknowledge that in an incredibly short period of time, Jack had completely claimed Adam's heart.

Oh, the kid was a lot of work. Didn't like to sleep. Went through enough diapers for a small army. But when he laughed, when he laid his head on Adam's shoulder, or patted his cheek with a gooey hand, it felt right.

"So," Sienna asked, "did you go out and conquer more of the planet today?"

One corner of his mouth lifted. He liked her attitude. Liked her smile. Her eyes. Her scent. Her taste. Hell.

"I did my share. What about you?" He moved into the room and sat down next to her. "Get all your pictures taken?"

"It was great," she said with a wide grin that lit up her eyes and made him want to take her mouth with his. "The park was perfect. And in the shots I got by the lake, I caught a flock of ducks swooping in. Caught them on the wing, with the trees bending in the wind and the blue sky and fat white clouds in the background."

She sighed in satisfaction. "That was perfect, but one of the kids got stuck in a tree and their father stepped in a mud hole, but all in all…"

Adam stared at her for a few seconds, then laughed. "Well, it's not the usual description of a workday."

"It's pretty usual for me." Jack leaned toward Adam, so Sienna handed the baby off to him.

Instantly, Jack slapped his banana-coated hands on the sleeves of Adam's pin-striped jacket. "Perfect."

"Oops." Sienna laughed, dug in the diaper bag for wipes and cleaned the baby's hands.

"A little late, but appreciated," Adam said wryly.

"Yeah, sorry." She wiped off his jacket sleeves and as she bent over, he could see down her shirt. He stared unabashedly and wished to hell he could touch her as easily as he could admire the view.

Gritting his teeth, he deliberately shifted his gaze and started talking to take his mind off what it really wanted to concentrate on. "The Explorer work for you?"

"I can't believe you gave me a brand-new car to drive around."

"I got it six months ago," he argued.

"He's still got that new car smell," she said, with a shake of her head.

"He?"

"Absolutely. No way is Thor a girl."

She sat up and Adam met her gaze. *"Thor?"*

"Well, he's burly and beautiful and there when I needed him." She grinned. "Besides, he just feels like a Thor to me."

"Right." Why Adam found her naming his car charming instead of just loony was beyond him. Shaking his head, he said, "Well you can use him—*it*—whenever you want."

"Thanks, I will until my car's fixed."

Yeah, they'd see about that. Her car was a nightmare. And all he'd had to do was disconnect the battery in "Gypsy" to make sure Sienna was driving something safe and reliable. He'd find a way to make the change permanent, too.

The baby jumped up and down on Adam's leg as if he were riding a horse, bringing Adam back to the situation at hand. "Kevin contacted a nanny employment agency."

"Oh." Sienna frowned a little. "Well, that's good, right?"

"Yeah," he said, nodding. "Hell, I didn't even know there *were* employment agencies strictly for nannies. Anyway, they have our requirements and they'll be sending people out for interviews. The first one is tomorrow."

"Tomorrow," she repeated, as if trying out the word. "Will you be interviewing them here?"

"Actually," he said, resettling Jack when the baby started trying to lurch forward, "I thought it'd be better if you talked to them first. Let whoever it is meet Jack at the house. See if it looks good. If you think it does, I'll do the final interviews." He met her gaze and wondered why all of a sudden he *couldn't* read what she was thinking. "Does that work for you?"

"Sure." She swallowed, took a breath and said, "That makes sense, really. I mean, if the baby doesn't like the nanny, we don't want her—or him—do we?"

"Right. That's what I was thinking. So, you'll be there tomorrow?"

"Yes. My next appointment isn't for a couple of days."

"Okay, great then." They sounded so stiff. Polite. A damn weird situation. Sienna was staying with him until he could find a nanny, and now that they had an appointment to interview one, neither of them was thrilled by the idea. Weird.

Jack squirmed on Adam's lap and reached out for Sienna. She scooped him up and stood.

Adam rose too and realized how much he liked that she was tall. Kissing her was easy, just a dip of his head and he could taste her again. He looked into her eyes and saw the same heat he felt swamping him. Like the night before, he shook his head and said, "This is crazy."

"I know," she said. "We weren't going to do anything about this." But her breath was coming faster and when she licked dry lips, Adam had to force himself not to take that mouth with his.

"We agreed it would be a mistake," he said, forcing each word from his throat.

She hitched the baby onto her hip, licked her lips again and whispered, "We already made one mistake. You know...when you..."

"Yeah." His memory of caressing her damp heat was seared into his brain. The feel of her when her body shuddered. The sound of her sighs and gasps. Bad move or not, it was something he hungered for. "Yeah, we did. And I want to do it all over again. And more."

"Oh me, too." She pulled in a long, slow breath. "But you said we were going to ignore it."

"I said we would *try* to ignore it."

She huffed out that breath. "How's that going for you?"

"Not good," he admitted.

"Me, either," she confessed.

He reached out and stroked one finger across the top of one of her breasts, then dipped into her cleavage and watched her eyes haze.

"Adam…" She shivered again and his body jolted in response.

He stopped touching her, pushed his hands through his hair. "We'll probably regret this."

"Maybe," she said, her gaze locked with his. "But I think I'd regret it more if we didn't make another 'mistake.'"

Now her eyes met his and he read her desire shining there. She wanted him. She wasn't being coy. Wasn't after his money or prestige or a first-class trip to Paris. Sienna was nothing like any woman he'd ever known. And right at that moment, he was grateful.

She wasn't playing games and he wouldn't, either.

Adam reached over and grabbed the diaper bag off the table. "Let's get out of here."

She blew out a breath, shook her hair back from her face and nodded, hitching the baby higher on her hip. "I'll take Jack in Thor and meet you at the house."

"Screw that." He wasn't taking the chance of her getting distracted on the drive home by another beach scene. He needed her and needed her *now.* "I'll get Kevin to bring my car to the house later. We'll both take Thor. Where did you park?"

"Just behind the building." He led her through the offices, waving off anyone who tried to get in his way. From the corner of his eye, he saw Kevin, and paused. "Kevin, I'm going home with Sienna. Have my car brought around, will you?"

"Sure." The man's smirk came and went so fast, only someone who knew Kevin as well as Adam did would have noticed it. Clearly, his best friend knew that Adam and Sienna were off to do exactly what Adam had insisted they wouldn't. "Have a good night. Nice to see you, Sienna."

"You too, Kevin. Hi to Nick." She said that last as the elevator doors closed between them. Looking up at Adam, she said, "Kevin knows why we're leaving together."

He glanced at her. "Does that bother you?"

She thought about it for a moment. "Maybe it should, but it doesn't."

"Good." He didn't want to waste any more time talking about or thinking about anything but what was bubbling between him and Sienna. The tension in the elevator was so thick it was hard to draw an easy breath. When the doors swished open, Adam herded Sienna and Jack along as quickly as he could.

In a few minutes, they had Jack secure and were driving down PCH. Traffic was thick. Even this early in the summer, beach lovers were crowding the coast. Teens with surfboards, moms with herds of kids, bikini-clad girls, they were all there and they were all contributing to slowing down the trip home.

The ride took forever but finally they pulled into the drive, only to see a white van with the slogan Tonight's The Night painted in black script on the side, parked in front of the house.

"Nick's here," Adam said on a groan. "You've got to be kidding me."

Glancing at Sienna, he expected to see the frustration he felt clearly marked on her features. Instead, her lips twitched, and then she laughed. An explosion of sound that rolled on and on as if she couldn't quite stop. In a second or two, Adam let go of the grinding aggravation lodged in his throat and smiled with her. Shaking his head, he said, "Maybe Somebody's trying to tell us something."

"Oh, I don't think Somebody bothers with the details of our lives."

"Well then, this is either a setup by Kevin or a weird coincidence."

Sienna laughed again and laid one hand on his forearm. He felt the heat shoot right down to his bones.

"Why would Kevin go out of his way to make sure we're interrupted?"

Thinking about his best friend and the man's sense of humor, Adam muttered, "He thinks he's funny."

"Well," Sienna said, "he is, usually. This? Not so much. Still, it'll be nice to see Nick."

From the back seat, Jack laughed, as if in on the joke, and Adam conceded that he'd lost this round. But he swore he'd get rid of Nick as fast as possible.

"How'd he get into the house?" Sienna asked as they unloaded the baby and all of his stuff.

"He and Kevin have an emergency key," he grumbled. "Which I'm seriously reconsidering."

Sienna laughed again as she headed for the house with the baby, and Adam followed, settling for watching the sway of her hips, telling himself that eventually, he was going to get his hands on her.

If the wanting didn't kill him first.

As soon as they opened the door, a blend of incredible scents greeted them.

Even Adam whispered, "Okay, it might be all right that Nick's here."

Grinning at him, Sienna started down the wide, tiled hall toward the kitchen, where they found Nick stirring a gleaming, stainless steel pot on the stove. When they stepped into the room, the big man spun around, took one look and shouted, "Sienna! It's so great to see you!"

Being hugged by Nick Marino was like being enveloped in warmth. He was tall and broad shouldered with the body of a weightlifter. He had once told her that working out was the only way he could combat all the calories he consumed having to taste everything he made before serving it. Nick's hair was black as night and held back in a short ponytail at the back of his head. His eyes were the deep brown of dark chocolate and his skin was burnished gold, revealing his love of the sun.

Sunlight poured through the windows, illuminating the white cabinets, the acres of forest green quartz and the honey-toned hardwood floors. There was a copper range hood over the stove and a copper faucet at the wide farmhouse sink. The windows offered an amazing view of the ocean and Sienna had already discovered that the sunsets from the balcony were incredible.

When Nick let her go, she smiled up at him. "I'm so happy to see you. Congratulations on the wedding."

"Thanks, sweetie. Married life is great." He stepped back and gave her a quick once-over. "You look spectacular."

Before she could answer, Adam asked, "What're you doing here, Nick?" and set the diaper bag on the kitchen counter.

"Well, Kevin told me about Sienna staying here for a couple of weeks—with no Delores to actually *cook*, so I took pity. I stuffed your freezer with enough fantastic dinners to last ten days. The rest of the time you can take Sienna *out* to dinner. Meanwhile, all you'll have to do is heat and eat, and then sigh in contentment." Nick winked. "Blessing my name, of course, for having saved you from canned soup and cheese sandwiches."

"You're the best," Sienna said, and jiggled Jack on her hip as he started to fuss.

Nick looked at the baby and his eyes went soft. "Devon's son." He lifted his gaze to Adam. "God, he looks just like him, doesn't he?"

"Yeah, he does."

Sienna didn't like the brief hint of sorrow she read in Adam's eyes, so she spoke up quickly and a little too brightly. "Do you want to hold him, Nick?"

Nick grinned. "You bet I do. I'm trying to talk Kevin into adopting, you know."

"I heard," Adam said knowingly.

Nick winced. "Yes, and I know you heard nothing wonderful. What I don't know is *why*. Kevin's great with kids. When his sisters bring their kids over, we all have a great time. I don't know why he's so hesitant." He lifted the baby and grinned when the tiny boy smiled at him.

"It's a big step," Sienna said with a shrug. "Takes some getting used to the idea, maybe."

"I wish he'd hurry up then." Nick did a fast turn to make the baby laugh in delight. A grin still plastered on his face, Nick glanced at Adam. "I called Kevin a few minutes ago to tell him I was here. He said to tell you that he was on his way with your car. That way he and I can just go home together."

"Kevin's on his way?" Adam asked, and sent her a glance that said, *See? I told you Kevin was behind this.*

"He is." Nick lifted the baby high in the air and giggles rained down on the room. "I've already got a lasagna in the oven, so we can all have dinner and visit for a while."

"Nick Marino's lasagna?" Sienna sighed. "No wonder it smells like heaven in here."

"Nick Marino Jameson, now," he told her with a quick grin.

She hugged him again. "I'll remember. So. Is there anything I can do to help?"

Nick winked at her. "Want to make a salad while I play with the little guy?"

"Sure."

"And Adam can pour us both some wine." Nick carried the baby into the adjoining den and did a few more spins just to hear little Jack laugh again.

Adam followed her to the fridge and leaned on the edge of the door when she opened it up.

"So much for great plans," he whispered, stroking the back of her hand with the tips of his fingers.

Funny—they'd gone from insane with desire and exploding passion into having dinner with friends, and still, he could make her sigh with a simple touch. She looked up into stormy brown eyes and said softly, "They won't be here all night."

"Damn right they won't. Even if I have to physically

toss Kevin out the door. We've still got 'mistakes' to make."

"Oh yes." She reached into the fridge and pulled out a bottle of wine. Handing it to him, she said, "I'm looking forward to it."

Nodding, he leaned in, took the wine and then brushed his mouth over hers. It was quick, hard and the taste of him lingered even after he pulled back. "I plan on making a *lot* of mistakes tonight."

Everything inside her quivered at the inherent promise in his tone, his eyes. "You're not making it easy to wait."

"Who wants easy?"

Nothing about this was the slightest bit easy, so she gave him a slow smile. "Clearly, neither of us." Taking a deep breath, she said, "Nick was right. I could use a glass of that wine."

"Or two," he said, and kissed her again.

"Hello? Wine steward?" Nick called from the other room.

Rolling his eyes, Adam muttered, "Can't catch a break here." Then to Nick, he spoke up. "It's coming, Your Majesty."

"Hey," Nick called back, "I like that."

"Of course you do." Shaking his head, Adam went for glasses.

Sienna laughed again and dug into the fridge for lettuce and vegetables. Passion could simmer through an evening with friends, she told herself, and maybe even make those feelings hotter, more desperate, for the wanting. Just thinking about what would come later made her blood sparkle like champagne.

Three hours later, Sienna realized she hadn't had so much fun in way too long. She'd been so busy the last couple of years, working on her business, staying focused, that she'd forgotten how good it was to simply *be*. Kevin entertained them all with stories about clients or the crews that worked for them. Nick's stories about the different catering jobs he'd done were just as entertaining. He and Sienna then commiserated with each other over how hard it was to establish a new business. And Adam made sure Kevin got plenty of one-on-one time with baby Jack—which Nick loved.

Sitting around the table in the big, beautiful kitchen, Sienna watched Adam with his friends and realized just how different he and Devon really had been. Devon had always had to be the star of the show. The entertainer. As if he thought no one would want to be with him if he wasn't constantly "on."

Adam didn't need to claim the center stage. The understated power of his presence, his personality, was enough. And now he seemed content to laugh at Nick's stories or argue with Kevin or to simply meet Sienna's gaze across the table and share a long, silent look.

As she'd suspected it would, rather than easing the desire that had been plaguing her for two days, this dinner with friends had only made it stronger. Watching Adam relaxed, laughing, had allowed Sienna to see him more clearly than she ever had before. The shields he usually kept up to protect himself were down and she felt as if she was getting to know the *real* Adam. So when Kevin and Nick finally left, Sienna was more than ready to make those mistakes they'd planned.

"I told you Kevin did that on purpose," Adam said. "Did you catch him smiling to himself when he first got here?"

"Yes. And I saw that you handed Jack off to him at every chance."

He shrugged and gave her a half smile. "Payback's a bitch. Besides, he's not as antikid as he wants Nick to think. I watched him with the baby tonight."

She looked up at him briefly as the white van's engine fired up. "So did I. He was having a good time."

"You can bet Nick saw it, too," Adam mused. The van headed down the driveway and they both waved until the taillights disappeared into the growing darkness.

Sienna had forgotten just how much she enjoyed Kevin. But after her divorce, she'd thought it best to stay away from all things Quinn. Which, unfortunately, had included Kevin and Nick. It seemed silly to her now, but at the time, she'd thought that keeping a distance was the right thing to do.

She smiled and gave him an elbow-nudge in the side. "They're so great. You're lucky to have them."

"Usually I feel that way. Tonight," he said, turning to wrap his arms around her, "I wished them halfway across the planet."

He pulled her in tightly to him and she felt the racing beat of his heart. Her own jumped into a gallop and she took a deep breath as she lifted her gaze to his. "They're gone now…"

He grinned down at her. "So they are."

"And the baby's asleep," she said softly, lifting her arms to hook them behind his neck. Nick had insisted on putting the baby down for the night and had even cajoled Kevin into helping him.

"News keeps getting better." He bent his head, took her mouth and stole her breath in the wash of heat that swamped her.

Sienna sighed as Adam's hands swept beneath the hem of her shirt, and up, along her spine. His fingers traced wild patterns on her skin as his tongue stroked her into a frenzy of need that clamored in her mind like fire alarms.

"Inside," he groaned when he tore his mouth from hers. "Inside, now, or I swear, we're going to do this on the porch."

She shivered and wondered if maybe she was a little bit of an exhibitionist, since that threat didn't sound so bad. She looked up into his eyes and saw his hunger, read the need etched into his features. "Yes," she said, and turned for the door. "Inside."

He was right behind her and when she would have headed for the stairs, he grabbed her hand and dragged her into the great room.

"Bedrooms are too far away," he muttered, and took her shirt, dragging it up and over her head. The cool air kissed her skin and her nipples went hard and erect when he undid her bra and pushed the straps down her arms to fall onto the floor.

"Beautiful," he whispered. "So damn beautiful." His hands cupped her breasts, his thumbs caressing her rigid nipples until she swayed on her feet, undone by what he was making her feel.

"You're driving me wild," she murmured, then gasped when he dipped his head to take first one nipple then the other into his mouth. Lips, tongue and teeth teased her sensitive skin until she whimpered in the back of her throat and half collapsed in his arms. Sienna knew that at any second, her knees were going to give out completely and she'd be in a puddle on the floor.

She didn't get the chance. Adam straightened up, tore off his shirt, then tipped her backward onto one of the couches. Sienna *whooped* in surprise, then grinned up at Adam as he tore off the rest of his clothes. She took a moment to relish the look of him, from his broad chest, long legs, narrow hips and *more*. Her eyes went wide in appreciation, and her stomach did a series of flips and spins in anticipation. She lifted her gaze to his and took a breath. "Well, hello..."

His eyes flashed and the faint smile curving his mouth faded in a blink. Eager now to feel all of him, she worked at the button and zipper of her jeans then pushed them and her panties down her legs to kick them off entirely. The couch was soft and cushioned and roomy enough for both of them to lie side by side. All she was interested in at the moment, though, was the man looming over her.

He covered her body with his and Sienna sighed at the simply delicious sensation of his bare, tanned skin brushing against hers. His chest was sharply sculpted muscle, telling her that he worked out regularly. She skimmed the flats of her hands across that expanse, loving the feel of him.

He smiled as he lowered his head to kiss her, tasting, teasing her lips with his tongue and teeth. She tried to catch his mouth with hers, but he managed to keep tantalizing her even as his hands swept up and down her body, exploring every line and curve. He slid one hand across her abdomen and down to the juncture of her thighs and Sienna braced herself for that first, magical touch.

She'd wanted to feel it again ever since that first night. Now, with his first caress, Sienna shivered in response. Sliding her hands up and down his back, over his shoulders and down his powerful arms, she indulged herself by touching him as he touched her. She ran one foot up his calf and sighed when he buried his head in the curve of her neck, tasting, nibbling. She tipped her head to one side to offer him access.

"God, you smell good," he murmured against her neck.

"Mmm, jasmine," she whispered.

"Tastes good, too," he said softly.

"Hope you're hungry…" She laughed when he nibbled at her neck, then sighed as his hands continued to caress every inch of her body. He lifted his head, looked down at her for what seemed forever, and then kissed her as if he were a dying man getting one last wish. Sienna held on to him, palms flat against his back. She opened her mouth for him and sighed at the sensual invasion of his tongue. Hers tangled with his and breathlessly, they chased each other up the rungs of sexual tension. Every second that ticked past, she felt her heartbeat quicken, her breath catch in her throat.

At the very heart of her, heat engulfed her. She wouldn't have been surprised to see actual flames dancing along her skin. A tingle of expectation dropped into the center of the fire and spun quickly out of control.

Arching up into him, Sienna met his kiss with a hunger that raged inside her. She'd waited for this. Maybe she'd been waiting since the very first time she'd met Adam. Her husband's brother. Out of bounds. Until now.

When he dropped one hand to the juncture of her thighs and cupped her heat again, she groaned. He pushed one finger, then two, into her depths and stroked her core until her hips rocked of their own accord. She surrendered control, arching into him, struggling, nearly screaming as tension built to an unbelievable height. Finally, she tore her mouth free of his and cried, "Adam, please. Inside me. Now."

"Now," he agreed. "I've got to have you." Adam shifted, then stopped. "Damn it."

"What? What? Why'd you stop?" She blinked wildly, trying to see through the passion-induced haze. Aching, needing, she demanded, "What's wrong?"

"Protection," he muttered grimly. "I'll be back. There are condoms upstairs."

"No!" She shook her head and grabbed his arm to keep him with her. "Don't go. I'm covered. I'm on the pill. And I'm clean."

He gave her a slow, satisfied smile. "I'm healthy, too."

"*Really* glad to hear it." Sienna pulled him closer. "Now, back to business."

"I admire a woman with a one-track mind…"

"You have no idea," she assured him.

Then all talk fled. Her mind, her soul, her body, were all too overwhelmed with sensation. Thinking, talking, were unnecessary and completely out of the question. She held her breath, lifted her hips and moaned when he entered her. Sienna gasped and held her breath as her body accommodated his. He felt right.

Then Adam went perfectly still and stared down into her eyes. Sienna read the passion shining down at her, and knew he was seeing the same thing in her eyes. Then he slowly began to move inside her, rocking his hips in a rhythm that quickly sent Sienna into a frenzy. She chased that tingle, raced after the flames. Her breath heaved in and out of her lungs. She moved with him in perfect tandem, as if they'd been born to come together in this ancient dance.

He pushed her higher, faster, and Sienna raced to keep up. She looked up into his eyes, saw the heat, saw the passion and lost herself in it. As her body peaked, she tumbled eagerly into the abyss opening up beneath her. Surrendering to the inevitable fall, Sienna trusted him to hold on to her. And when he shouted her name and fell with her, she closed her eyes and savored the crash.

Eight

By the time her heartbeat was back to normal, Sienna's brain was working again. The feel of Adam's body on hers, the brush of his ragged breath against her neck, combined to create a satisfied sigh that slipped from her throat.

Adam lifted his head, looked down into her eyes and smiled. "I don't make mistakes often," he admitted, "but this one was well worth it."

Sienna lifted one hand and stroked his hair back from his face. In the darkness, his eyes shone down at her. He was still buried deep inside her body and she felt as if even their souls were touching. She couldn't remember another time when she felt such a connection to someone. Yet, as he'd just said, it had been a mistake. And though it had been wonderful, Sienna knew that she also had to consider this time with him a major slip in judgment.

But her mouth curved as she spoke on a sigh. "It was right up there for me, too. Top two at least."

He shifted, pulling away from her, sitting up and grabbing his clothes. It seemed, she thought with a sinking heart, the moment was over. Since she was at a distinct disadvantage naked, Sienna picked up her clothes, as well. She swung her hair out of her face, tugged her jeans on and shrugged into her shirt.

God, her body felt loose and relaxed, while inside she was a churning mess of mixed emotions and feelings that she would worry about sorting out later and— She caught him looking at her through narrowed eyes. "What?"

"You seem happy."

Funny, she thought. The first time he was wrong in reading her expression. But she went with it, because why admit to being so confused?

"Why wouldn't I be?" She lifted both arms over her head and stretched.

His frown deepened and she had to wonder when exactly Mr. Sexy had become Mr. Crabby. Was he feeling as torn as she was? "What's going on, Adam?"

"I just don't want you to get the wrong idea, that's all." His dark eyes were completely shut down. He could have been a robot for all the emotion she read there. How did he do that so quickly? So completely?

Tipping her head to one side, she stared up at him. "What wrong idea?" she asked. "Be specific."

He glanced around the room as if checking to make sure they were alone—after what they'd just done, they'd better be, Sienna thought. Then he turned his gaze back to her. "I was married before," he blurted.

"Hey, me, too." Frowning a little, she asked, "This is not a news flash. So where are you going with this, Adam?"

He pushed one hand through his hair. "I just want you to know up-front, that I'm not looking to get married again."

Stunned, she could only blink at him as her mind raced to figure out where *that* had come from. Nope, she acknowledged a moment later, couldn't do it. "Did I propose or something in the throes of passion?" Sarcasm colored her tone. "Because that would just be tacky."

He blew out a breath, scrubbed one hand across his face and said, "It's not a joke, Sienna."

"I'm not laughing, Adam." In fact, she'd never felt less amused. Did he really think she'd had sex with him just to trick him somehow into marrying her? Did he think she'd done that to *Devon*?

"No point in getting mad. I just want us to know the lay of the land right from the start," Adam said.

"Devon swept you off your feet and into a marriage. That's not going to happen with me."

"Well, good. I didn't ask to be swept," she reminded him, letting the first bubble of anger rising in her chest grow and swell. Damn it. "If you think I somehow seduced Devon into marrying me, you're wrong. And you're even *more* wrong if you believe I've got some nefarious plan to snag *you*."

"Sienna..."

"Believe me when I say that you can relax, Adam. You're completely safe from the gold-digging femme fatale."

"I didn't say that," he blurted out.

Her gaze fired into his. "Do you realize how often you say those words? 'I didn't say that.' It's like your mantra or something. Maybe you should get some calling cards printed with that phrase so you can hand them out to everyone you manage to insult without even trying."

"Sienna—"

"Or you know what?" She walked closer to him and poked him in the chest with her index finger. "Instead of overusing that one particular phrase and confusing everyone around you, maybe instead you should rethink the things you *do* say *before* you say them."

"You don't sound confused." He glanced down at her finger, still jabbing at his chest, then up into her eyes again. "You sound mad."

"You'll be happy to know that your powers of perception are still A+. Congratulations, Adam."

"I'm not trying to make you angry—"

Her head snapped back and her eyes went wide. "Wow, and look how well you're doing without any effort at all." Sienna folded her arms across her chest and tapped the toe of one bare foot against the rug. Amazing that he could stir her up as easily as he did. Passion. Fury. Befuddlement.

He was always so damn sure of himself. And apparently convinced that he was such a magnificent catch that any woman who wormed her way into his bed was there for the express purpose of making it permanent. She took several deep breaths in an attempt to keep her head from exploding.

His gaze was still detached. Cool, while she was burning hot. Adam was always so positive that his way was the right way he would never be dissuaded by temper. Hers or anyone else's. Now logic, on the other hand, might just get through.

"I just want us both to be clear on what this is," Adam said tightly.

Deliberately, she pushed her anger aside and focused instead on convincing the man that he was being an idiot. An insulting idiot.

"Oh, I'm perfectly clear on that. It seems to me that *you're* the one having an issue. This is *sex*, Adam. It's not a declaration of forever. It's passion, desire." Shaking her head, she let the last of her fury fade because in his own completely stupid way, he was trying to be fair to her. "We're both adults. Why can't we just be together until it's over, and then walk away friends?"

Now it was his turn to simply stare at her as if she were speaking Martian. Sienna almost laughed in spite of the situation. Irritation smoothed out. Honestly, she found she really liked being able to confuse him. Obviously, the women he was accustomed to weren't quite as forthright as she was.

"Friends."

"Why not?" she asked. A part of her mind was shrieking *You'll never be his friend*, but she ignored that and moved in closer to him. Sliding her palms up his bare chest, pushing back the open edges of his shirt, she felt his heart pounding. However cool he wanted to act, she knew he was feeling more than he pretended, and somehow, that cheered her up a little. Staring up into his eyes, she said, "Just stop thinking, Adam. And for heaven's sake, stop talking."

A moment or two passed before a smirk lifted one corner of his mouth. "I've never had a woman tell me to shut up before."

She grinned back at him. How could she not? He was everything Devon hadn't been. Everything she'd ever really wanted and he wasn't hers. Wasn't going to *be* hers. Except for now. For whatever stolen time they had together before it ended and the world returned to normal.

"Well then," she said, "I'm proud to be the first."

"Of course you are." He shook his head, gave her a wry smile, then cupped her face in his palms and bent his head to kiss her. Just before he did, he paused and said, "So lovers now, *friends* later."

Sienna's blood began to boil again. "We can be friends now, too, if you want."

"No, thanks." His smile faded. "What I want to do to you, I don't do to my friends."

She quivered, told herself to enjoy every moment of her time with him and leaned in close. "Show me."

He did.

Adam wasn't used to waking up with company.

He didn't spend the night with any woman and he sure as hell didn't let them stay over at his house. That way led to too many assumptions. In his experience, once a woman stayed over, she tended to think more proprietarily. Soon, there'd be little things left behind, as if she were marking her territory. So it was easier—and more honest—to end the night early and sleep alone.

So what the hell had happened to that rule last night?

Yes, Sienna was staying at the house anyway, but staying in his bed was different. She was still sleeping, her blond hair a tangle across her face. Her eyelashes lay like silk fans on her cheeks and the pale gray sheet covering her body dipped over one breast, as if tempting him to taste her.

Dawn was just streaking the sky with ribbons of rose and gold, turning the dusky light to soft lavender. Adam went up on one elbow to look down at her. With the tips of his fingers, he lifted a strand of her hair, then bent to kiss her bare shoulder. Soft. Naked. Sienna.

She sighed and instinctively moved closer to him. All night, they'd had each other. Fast, slow and everything in between. He couldn't seem to get enough of her. Every touch only fed the need for more. Every climax made him burn hotter.

Friends, she'd said last night. Adam almost laughed. He didn't want to be her friend. And temporary lover wasn't enough. But what was left? Anything beyond temporary wasn't in his game plan.

And Adam always kept to the damn plan. Knowing where he was going, what he was doing, kept him focused on his goals. But with Sienna, he felt as if he were always a step behind. He didn't like it.

That said, he liked everything else about her. Her wit. The stinging sarcasm and the way she stood up for herself. Her scent. Her taste.

He bent his head, took that tantalizing nipple into his mouth and as he suckled her, he felt her wake. She threaded her fingers through his hair, held his head to her and gasped, "Good morning."

He smiled against her breast, then lifted his head to look down at her. Even first thing in the morning, not a drop of makeup, her hair wild from sleep and sex, she was the most beautiful thing he'd ever seen.

"It is now," he said, and rolled her over onto her back. Moving to cover her body with his, he parted her thighs and slipped inside her before she could take another breath. Warmth spilled through his veins as he watched her take him. Her eyes closed briefly on another sigh, then she opened them and fixed her gaze on his. Adam thought wildly that he could drown in the blue of her eyes and it wouldn't be a bad way to go.

And then the rhythm caught them, held them. In the soft hush of dawn, he watched her eyes glaze with the kind of heat that torched everything inside him. She lifted her legs and locked them around his hips, pulling him tighter, deeper. Their gazes locked, they watched each other as the end rushed toward them.

The morning light brightened and her eyes glittered fiercely. "Go over," he whispered, controlling his own need in favor of watching her shatter first. "Go and I'll follow."

She arched her head back, closed her eyes, and he felt her body clench around his. Digging her short, neat nails into his shoulders, she cried out his name and let the internal explosions take her.

Adam felt her pleasure as his own and knew that she was touching something inside him no one else ever had. What it meant for him, for *them*, he didn't know. And when his own release claimed him an instant later, he didn't care. All that mattered was the woman in his arms and the silent clock in his mind, slowly counting off their days together.

A few hours later, Sienna was exhausted. She was working on about two hours' sleep and though her body felt wonderfully well used, she really needed a nap. That was not in the cards though, as she went back and forth between caring for Jack and working on her laptop. Doing the drudge work of owning your own business was time-consuming and less than fun. She went through the bills, paying some, delaying others. She looked up her calendar and made notes about what she wanted to do on the photo shoots.

And finally, she welcomed her creative side and pulled up her digital files. Going through the images she took in Central Park the other day, she made some corrections, some deletions, then turned to editing and got lost in refining her favorite shots. And she did it all on way too little sleep.

Which was probably why the nanny interview didn't go well.

"Thanks for coming by, Ms. Stryker," she said, Jack cuddled close to her chest.

Evangeline Stryker was tall, thin with a sharp blade of a nose and ice-blue eyes. Middle-aged with a ramrod-straight posture, she was, in fact, the cliché of a mean governess. All she needed was a wart on her chin and a hideous cackle. Sienna felt a little guilty

for the thought, but then the woman spoke again and
her English was so precise, Sienna felt like a peasant
before a grumpy duchess.

"I appreciate your time. If I am hired, I can assure
you that the child will receive care and discipline."
The older woman reached out toward Jack and the
baby cringed like a vampire from a cross.

The child. Sienna smothered a sigh. Ms. Stryker
was perfectly qualified, but seemed cold and Jack
hadn't taken to her at all. So that was a no go on the
nanny front.

The woman's eyebrows arched high on her forehead and her disapproval was evident. Oh well.
"Again, thanks for coming."

"Certainly." As the nanny walked across the drive
to her sedate black sedan, Cheryl arrived in her VW
bug. The bright yellow car was like a splotch of sunshine in the grimness, and right then, Sienna really
needed it.

Cheryl climbed out of her car wearing jeans, flip-
flops and a pink, button-down shirt. Her short, dark
hair was a perfect bob at her jawline and the purse
she carried slung over one shoulder was almost as
big as she was.

Giving the nanny a quick look as she passed,
Cheryl gave a dramatic shudder, then grinned. When
she walked close enough, she said, "Hi, who's that?"

"A would-be nanny," Sienna told her as the woman
drove away.

"Oh, don't do that to this sweet cutie." Cheryl plucked Jack into her arms and the baby laughed and slapped her cheeks. Okay, Cheryl had the stamp of approval, which just proved that Jack was a baby of discernment.

"So." Cheryl gave Sienna a hard stare. "You had sex."

"What?" Was it stamped on her forehead?

"Please, am I blind?" Cheryl hooked her arm through Sienna's and pulled her into the house. "Tell me *everything*. But first, a tour." She craned her neck to look around the hall and into the great room. "I have to see this place."

An hour later, the tour was over and Cheryl was feeding Jack in the kitchen while Sienna sipped coffee.

"And now," she said, "I've got to find a nanny."

"Why you?" Cheryl asked. "Jack is Adam's nephew. He should be doing the interviewing."

"That's what I thought at first, too," Sienna admitted, practically inhaling the caffeine. "But he had a point. Whoever gets hired will be living here. Taking care of Jack. So why shouldn't they come here first? See how the baby reacts to them—and Jack did not like Ms. Stryker."

"Good for him," Cheryl said, leaning forward to plant a quick kiss on Jack's forehead. "She even scared *me*."

"Me, too, a little." Sienna yawned and Cheryl gave her a knowing smile.

"Busy night?"

"Jealous?"

"Desperately."

"You should be."

"Oh," Cheryl said, "that's just mean. So if you're this tired, why don't you look happier?"

"Because it's…complicated," Sienna admitted, getting up to refill her cup.

"All the best things are," Cheryl said.

She looked at her friend, sitting in the sunshine-filled kitchen. Then her gaze fixed on the laughing baby slapping both hands against the tray of his high chair. Sunlight gilded his hair and sparkled in his eyes and Sienna's heart squeezed.

"You're falling in love," Cheryl said softly.

"What?" Sienna jolted, shook her head and said, "No, I'm not. Adam and I are just…*not*, that's all."

"Interesting," Cheryl said, smirking at her. "I meant you were falling in love with this baby. But it's fascinating how you went straight to Adam…"

Sienna closed her eyes and sighed. "Don't start."

"I didn't start it—I just remarked on it. Isn't that right, Jack?"

The baby giggled and Sienna sighed again. "Fine. Maybe I feel a little more for Adam than I want to admit to."

"Blatantly obvious, and…?"

"And, nothing," Sienna said firmly. "This is temporary, Cheryl. Once I find a nanny and a place for Adam to renovate for my business, then this is over."

Cheryl wiped the baby's face, and then gave Sienna a long look. "Do you *want* it to be over so soon?"

"Doesn't matter what I want, does it?"

"Of course it matters," Cheryl snapped. "What are we, in the Middle Ages or something? If you want him, go get him."

"You make it sound easy."

"It's not," Cheryl said. "But it's also not impossible. Let him know you're interested in more."

Sienna shook her head firmly and folded both hands around her coffee cup. "No. He already gave me the 'don't get any ideas' speech."

"He did not."

Sienna just looked at her. "Yes, he did. But he didn't have to. I knew going in that he wasn't interested in more than *now*. And I assured him that I'm fine with that. That I'm not looking to be swept away into a romance."

Cheryl gave her a smile. "But you are?"

"I don't know," she said, then added, "I mean I do know, but no, I'm not, even though I am, because there's nothing waiting for me there but the Valley of Pain."

"That was completely convoluted and I still got it." Cheryl reached over and gave Sienna's hand a pat. "All I'm saying is, if you found something you want, go for it."

"Even if there's no hope of getting it?"

"The only way you absolutely cannot have something is if you never try."

While her friend lifted Jack out of the high chair, Sienna wondered. She thought about spending time with Adam the last few days. The laughter, the conversations, the kisses and then, oh, my, *last night*. She felt as if he'd been branded into her skin and she really wanted to do it all again. As soon as possible.

Waking up with him that morning, him sliding deep inside her, Sienna had felt a sense of completion she'd never known before. They shared so much and at the same time, they were so far apart. And that's how it should stay, for her own good.

Deliberately, Sienna reminded herself that once she found a nanny and a building for her photography business, their relationship would be over.

And with that thought in mind, she opened her eyes, looked at Cheryl and said, "Want to go for a ride? I need to find the perfect photo studio."

She didn't expect to find something so quickly, but an hour later, Sienna knew she'd stumbled on the perfect property. On the outskirts of Long Beach, the Craftsman had probably been built in the forties. It boasted a wide front porch with stone columns, windows that overlooked Ocean Avenue and beyond that, the sea. It was surrounded by other old homes that had been turned into law offices, art galleries and even a ceramics shop.

"It'll take a lot of work," Cheryl mused.

"True, but when it's finished..." Problems with Adam momentarily forgotten Sienna grabbed her camera to take a quick picture of the For Sale sign, to get the agent's phone number.

Once that was taken care of, Sienna said, "You know, as long as we're here in Long Beach, we could stop by my place, pick up my long lens. I want to get some shots of the view off Adam's balcony."

"That's not all you want off Adam's balcony..."

"Seriously?" Sienna laughed and shook her head. Sadly, the action didn't shake the image of her and Adam on a chaise on that balcony out of her mind.

"I'm with you." Cheryl settled back in her seat. "Mike's got the kids and I have the afternoon off."

"Great. We'll go to my house, then maybe stop for a coffee and brownie?"

"Now you're talking."

Sienna shot a quick look at Jack, sleeping peacefully in his car seat, then she put Thor in gear and headed for her home. Ten minutes later, she was parked in the driveway staring at a house she didn't recognize.

"Wow," Cheryl said from beside her, "when did you do all of this? And why didn't you tell me?"

Sienna climbed out of Thor and spared her friend

a glance. "I didn't do it. Adam did. And he didn't tell *me*."

"Uh-oh."

"Damn right." Her gaze swung back to her house and she struggled to take it all in. The house was now sky blue with bright white trim. The porch was painted a navy blue and she had to admit, through her fury, that it really added something to the curb appeal.

Her ancient front door now boasted a high-gloss finish of sunshine-yellow paint and there were even fresh flowers potted on the porch. She took a longer look at the place. Her front walk had been replaced. The cracks were gone. Even the one that looked like the Big Dipper.

Plus, she could tell at a glance that Adam had replaced her roof and there was a brand-new garage door complete with stained glass inserts along the top. The whole place looked like an old woman who'd been given a makeover by the best in the business. You could still tell her age, but she looked shiny.

Cheryl got out of the car, walked around and stood beside her. "How did he get all of this done so fast?"

Good question. He must have put a crew on her house the day she agreed to help him out. Well, she hadn't asked him to do it, had she?

"What was he thinking?" Sienna demanded, not really expecting an answer. "He didn't ask me if it was okay to do this. No, not Adam Quinn. He just decides something needs fixing and he does it."

"Well hell, he should be shot," Cheryl said sharply.

Sienna shot her an exasperated look. "This is *my* house, Cheryl. Not his."

"And now it looks like it won't blow over in the next wind." Cheryl looked at her. "Didn't you lose like thirty shingles in last winter's big storm, and then spend the next few nights emptying pots of rainwater?"

Remembering the nights filled with the plops and drops made her bite back a groan. Naturally, when her roof was leaking, they got near Biblical rains. "Yes," she agreed. "But that's not the point—"

"Didn't you tell me you were going to have the roof repaired this summer?"

"Yes…"

"So now it's done."

And it looked beautiful. Blue shingles. Of course Adam would think about details like that. Irritating man. "But I didn't do it. *He* did."

"Bonus, if you ask me, which you didn't."

"You don't get it," Sienna said, whipping her head back to glare at the high-gloss yellow paint on her front door. She really loved that and it went perfectly with the navy porch and the white trim and— Irritating man. "He did it because he clearly doesn't think I'm capable of taking care of my own life."

Cheryl snorted. "Oh, come on. Maybe he's just a nice guy."

"Nice guys bring you flowers. They don't put a new roof on your house."

"They do if they're *rich* nice guys," Cheryl said.

"No." Sienna shook her head. "No, I have to make him stop or he'll run right through the rest of my life. He's already got me living at his house, driving his car, taking care of his nephew and picking out buildings that he can renovate for me."

"Again. Call the executioner."

Scowling at her friend, Sienna muttered, "You're on his side."

"In this, so far, yeah," Cheryl said, and leaned in to check on the still-sleeping baby. "From what I can see, he's fixed your house, agreed to give you a fabulous new office and he's provided sex great enough to put a glow on your face. How is any of that a bad thing?"

When she put it like that, it was hard to argue. But Sienna's pride kept throttling her. How could she let Adam do all of this without so much as discussing it with her?

"I have to talk to him," Sienna muttered.

Cheryl sighed. "Of course you do. Okay then, go in and get your lens, then you can take me to get my car before you face Adam."

"Fine." A few minutes later, Sienna climbed into Thor and turned the key. She was so furious she didn't even enjoy the purr of the engine. "He's got to stop, Cheryl."

"Good luck with that, sweetie," her friend said as she got in and buckled her seat belt. "In my experience, it's easier to move a mountain than it is to get a man to do what you want him to do."

She had a point, Sienna told herself as she backed out of her newly asphalted driveway. How had she missed *that* when she pulled in?

"Maybe you're right," Sienna said thoughtfully. "But Adam is going to learn that it's not easy to bulldoze Sienna West."

Nine

By the time Sienna dropped Cheryl off, and then made the trek back to Adam's office, her initial anger had burned off. But the irritation bar was still pretty high.

Walking through the office with Jack on her hip, Sienna smiled and nodded to everyone, then stopped at Kevin's desk.

"Well hi," he said, giving her a quick glance up and down. "You look gorgeous."

Surprised at the compliment, Sienna took a quick look down at herself. She'd completely forgotten that she was wearing a simple summer dress and high-heeled red sandals. She'd wanted to look nice for the nanny interview, and then simply hadn't bothered to change later.

"Oh, thanks. Um, is Adam free?"

"He just finished up a meeting, so yes." Kevin stood up as if to walk her to Adam's office. "You caught him at a good time."

"Great. Here. Will you watch Jack for a few?" She handed the baby off without giving the man a chance to object. "He should be fine, but there are diapers and bottles in the bag."

Kevin looked wildly panicked for a second, but Sienna was on a mission and couldn't take the time to soothe the man. She did, however, manage to say in exasperation, "He doesn't bite."

"We'll see…" Warily, Kevin held the tiny boy, who laughed at him in delight.

Sienna had already turned, heading for the set of double doors leading into the lion's den. She opened one, stepped inside the inner sanctum and closed the door behind her. For just a moment, she leaned back against the doors and stared at the big man across the room, sitting behind a wide desk.

Adam wore a charcoal-gray suit with a black shirt and a bloodred tie. He looked every inch exactly what he was. A power broker. A rich, successful man who ran the world around him exactly as he wanted to.

Sunlight poured in from behind him, gilding him in a way that made it look as if the office had been designed to showcase Adam as the absolute ruler. Her stomach did a quick spin and dip in automatic reaction to him, before she reminded herself that she was here because Adam thought he could run *her* world, too.

He caught her eye and gave her a slow smile that made her toes curl. "Well, hello. You look beautiful."

She really should wear a dress more often.

"Thank you." He was disarming her with a compliment and a smile that hinted of wicked thoughts and even more wicked deeds. Damn it. "Adam, I went by my house this afternoon—"

He leaned back in his chair, comfortable. In charge. "Yeah? What'd you think? I haven't seen it in person, but Toby Garcia took some pictures when it was finished. Looked good to me."

She blinked at him. Sienna had expected defensiveness. The King of the Universe tone saying something along the likes of *Too bad if you're not happy, I wanted it done and it's done.* Instead… "It's beautiful, but—"

"Glad you liked it." He slapped both hands on the arms of his chair. "I thought the garage door was nice."

"Yes," she said, remembering how elegant the arched windows along the tops of the door looked. "The stained glass is gorgeous, but—"

He stood up, came around the desk and walked toward her in long, lazy strides. "It's a thirty-year roof, too. So you won't have to worry about leaks anymore."

This was *not* going how she'd thought it would go. "That's great, Adam—"

"Kevin chose the yellow paint for the door. I

wanted a bright red, but he said the yellow would contrast better."

Kevin had a good eye, because that bright yellow made the whole house just *sing*. "Yes, it's gorgeous."

He was so close now she could see her own reflection in his eyes. She looked confused. Hardly surprising since not only had he taken the wind out of her anger sails, he actually had her complimenting him on the work they'd done.

"It was Toby's idea to lay down new asphalt on the driveway, but I think it was a good call."

"Sure. Toby who?"

"Garcia. He's the crew chief."

She'd have to find him. Tell him what a good job they'd all done. *For heaven's sake, Sienna, you were mad, remember?*

"Right, well the driveway's nice, but—"

"And with the new walkway to the porch," he continued, "you won't trip and break your neck."

She'd tripped on those cracks more than once, but she didn't have to admit to that. Besides, "The Big Dipper's gone."

"What?"

Sienna sighed as she realized that she'd not only lost the upper hand, she didn't have a clue where it had gone. "One of the cracks looked like the Big Dipper."

He snorted. "Only you would see the stars by looking *down*."

Sienna took a deep breath. "Adam, I came here to tell you that you can't do this kind of thing."

"Too late," he said, one corner of his mouth quirking. "It's already done."

And there it was. Exactly what she'd expected to hear. "See, you're not even sorry."

"Why would I be sorry?" He looked bemused at the very idea.

"Because you didn't bother to consult me when you decided to do a makeover on *my* house?"

He shook his head and waved that away with one hand. "You would have said no."

How were you supposed to win a battle with a man who used that kind of logic? "Exactly."

"So we avoided that argument and the work's done."

Dumbfounded, she stared up into his eyes and saw a flash of amusement that really should have made her angry. But what would have been the point? He was right. The work was already done, no reason to argue about it now. And she really hated that she loved what he'd done to her house, too. Hard to maintain righteous indignation when a part of her was thinking *Ooooohhh...* But he knew that. Had counted on it. And Sienna didn't like being played, either.

"Don't do something like that again, Adam."

"Do you own another home?"

"No."

"Then no problem," he said amiably. "Although…" He walked back to his desk, picked up a folder, then came back to her. "You should probably just take this now."

She frowned and stared at the folder as if it were a snake. Sienna was wary now, so she asked, "What is it?"

He shrugged. "The pink slip to the Explorer. Car's been signed over to you."

"What?" She gaped at him. Sienna knew she must have looked like a landed trout, with her eyes bugged out and her mouth hanging open in shock, but she couldn't help it. "No, you didn't—"

He shook the folder in an imperious manner until she instinctively reached out to take it. Then helplessly she opened it to see all the paperwork. A pink slip. The insurance paperwork and cards. Registration. Shaking her head, she lifted her gaze to his. "You're crazy. I don't need Thor. I already have a car."

"No you don't. You have a metal doorstop shaped like a car."

Insulted on Gypsy's behalf, Sienna stiffened. "You can't just do this."

"Why not?" Again, he sounded completely sincere. As if it were a usual thing for a person to give another person an amazing SUV free and clear.

"Because—" She reached for words. For outrage. For *something*. And came up empty. Finally, she settled for, "I don't want you to."

"Oh, well, if that's all..." He gave her a lopsided grin that tugged at everything she was.

God, she really loved that smile. She shook her head firmly. "Adam, seriously, you have to stop this."

"Sienna," he said on a long exhalation of breath, "this is all your fault, anyway."

"What?" There was that word again. She laughed and heard just a tinge of hysteria. "How is this my fault?"

"You're the one who named the car Thor. I can't even get into the thing now. It'd be like sitting in the lap of a huge guy with long blond hair and a hammer."

She laughed again. "That's ridiculous."

"You painted the mental picture," he said slowly, "I just see it."

Sienna took a deep breath and let it out again. "So you expect me to just accept a new car—*and* everything you did to my house."

"Yes."

"Why is it so hard to argue with you?"

He shrugged. "Because you know I'm right?"

She shook her head. "No, I don't think that's the reason." Staring up into his eyes, she said, "Before I saw the house, before you gave me a *car*, I was going to tell you that I found a place for the photography studio."

"Yeah?" His face brightened and curiosity shone in his eyes. "That's great."

"Yes, well, now I don't think I'm comfortable with our deal. You've already done too much for me— doesn't even matter that I didn't ask you to."

"You can't back out of our deal, Sienna." He reached out and rubbed his hands up and down her bare arms. And it felt like a match touched to kindling.

"Adam…"

"You know, I really like this dress."

"Oh." He threw her off deliberately. She was beginning to think he enjoyed it. "Thanks. I wanted to look good to interview the nanny who didn't work out anyway, so—"

"Let's not waste that dress."

She was almost afraid to ask, "What do you mean?"

"Do you have your camera with you?"

"Of course. It's in Thor."

"Naturally." He took her arm and steered her out of his office. "Okay, let's go."

"Go where?"

"First to the place you found—"

"Adam we have to talk about that."

"—then to Dana Point. You can take those pictures of our new project."

They walked into the big outer office and stopped dead. Kevin was playing peekaboo with Jack. The baby laughed, Kevin grinned, then looked sheepishly over at Adam when the man cleared his throat.

"Fine," Kevin said. "You caught me. I don't actually hate babies. Don't tell Nick."

"He knows," Sienna said, and smiled to herself. She had a feeling Kevin was going to stop fighting the idea of adoption. That should make Nick happy.

"Glad you're having a good time." Adam kept a firm grip on Sienna as he said, "Keep it up. Take Jack back to my place, will you? You can drive the Explorer—the car seat's in it. I'm taking Sienna down to Dana Point to get some shots of the wave project."

Kevin shrugged. "Sure. I can do that."

She was being steamrolled—again—but for some reason it wasn't bothering her. Sienna was starting to worry about that.

"If you get hungry," she said, "Nick left some meals in the freezer."

Grinning, Kevin said, "If I get hungry, I'll call Nick and get him to come over and feed me."

"That works, too. We'll get dinner out, so you and Nick enjoy yourselves," Adam said, already walking away. Sienna looked over her shoulder at Kevin, who gave her a thumbs-up as she hurried to keep pace with Adam.

She had no idea how she'd lost control of this confrontation. She had gone there to lay down the law and instead, she was being swept off on an adventure. She threw him a quick, sideways glance as they stepped into an elevator. He was so damn bossy. Why did she find that so attractive?

"I didn't say I'd go to dinner with you," she said.

He looked down at her and smiled. "I didn't ask."

"I can't believe you did that."

Adam watched her from across the table and relished the mixture of excitement and bafflement in her eyes. "You keep saying that," he said. "But you were there. You heard the conversation."

"I know." She picked up her glass of wine, took a sip, then shook her head.

That action sent her long hair sliding back and forth across her shoulders in a sinuous movement that was hypnotizing. Adam's breath caught in his chest until it felt like he might explode from the pressure.

"It's just," Sienna said for at least the third time, "I've never heard of someone calling a real estate agent and making a cash offer on a house they haven't even inspected."

"You have to let that go."

"I don't think I can." She laughed a little helplessly. "I don't think the agent's going to recover anytime soon, either."

"Yeah," he said, remembering how the woman had sputtered and gasped over the phone. He shrugged and took a long drink of his wine. "Look, bottom line? You found what you wanted. Good spot for it. Lots of walk-in traffic and drive-bys will see you easily. Plenty of room, and the house itself has good bones. Once we get the deed, we'll take a walk through and you can tell me exactly what you want."

"You mean I get to have input this time?"

One corner of his mouth lifted. "That was the deal."

The restaurant was crowded, even so early. They

had a table by the glass, with a view of the cliffs below and the surf pounding against the rocks as steady as a heartbeat. There were candles on the tables, weeping violins pumping through the stereo system and the most beautiful woman he'd ever known sitting across from him.

She wore a summer dress that was a soft, white fabric with dark red flowers scattered all over it. Wide straps curved over her shoulders and a square bodice drew attention to her breasts without displaying them. The skirt was full and hit just above her knees and the high-heeled red sandals she wore showcased shiny red toenails. Her long blond hair was loose and caressing her skin with every tiny movement. Her smile, when she looked at him, lit up her face and shone in her eyes.

And damn it, Adam felt something. He didn't want to admit it—hell, even think about it. But it was there.

She was encroaching too deeply into his life. His world. Thoughts of her were constantly swimming through his mind, and when he was anywhere near her, all he could think about was getting her naked and losing himself in her arms, her heat, her eyes.

Warning bells went off in his mind, but Adam was too far gone to listen. Sienna crossed her long, tanned legs and claimed his full attention. She was too beautiful. Too talented. Too funny. Too damn smart. She was too much of everything, which meant he'd been with her too long.

He needed some space. And not just from Sienna. He needed room to seriously think about Jack. Yes, he loved the baby, but that didn't mean he'd be any damn good at raising him. He needed help, and so far the nanny situation wasn't working out. Sienna had told him on the drive about how their first applicant had had mean eyes and made Jack cry. What the hell was he supposed to do with *that*?

Good thing he had a trip to Santa Barbara coming up. He could get away. Think. Try to make sense of what was happening in his life.

"Adam?" The tone of her voice told him it wasn't the first time she'd spoken to him.

"Sorry. What?"

"Are you okay?"

No, he wasn't okay at all. But damned if he was going to confess that to the woman who was the *reason* his usually centered, logical mind was suddenly going off on tangents.

"I'm just thinking." Frowning, he said, "You didn't like that nanny. I talked to the owner of the agency today and she sounded so cold I damn near got frostbite over the phone."

She frowned, too. "That doesn't sound good."

"No," he admitted. "It doesn't. I'm thinking now that maybe Delores was onto something when she offered to care for Jack."

"Really?" Candlelight reflected in her eyes.

"For now, anyway," he said. Actually it had only just occurred to him a few minutes ago. But the more he thought about Sienna, the more he wanted her—and the more he knew he had to get her out of his life. He was getting drawn in too deep and he couldn't allow that.

So if Delores took care of the baby, then as soon as she came back from vacation, this time with Sienna would end. They wouldn't be together even longer, searching for some mythical nanny they might *never* find. If they did that, this thing between them could drag on forever and he'd get pulled deeper and deeper into something he knew damn well would never work out.

Better to end it now. For her sake, he reminded himself.

"Well, good." She lifted her glass again. "So no more interviews?"

"Not necessary. Delores will be back in a little over a week. If you can stay until then, I'd appreciate it." He told himself to be polite. Businesslike. No point in making this ugly as he worked to end it. He wouldn't be her friend. He couldn't continue to be her lover. Didn't mean he had to be her enemy, though.

Confusion etched itself into her features. "I thought we'd already decided that I would stay."

"Okay. That's good. Thanks."

Don't look at the rise and fall of her breasts. Ignore it when she licks her bottom lip.

He'd have to tell her that what was between them was over. But damned if he'd do that to her over dinner.

He already knew he was terrible at relationships. And his brother had already caused Sienna enough grief for one lifetime. So really, he would be doing this—*ending* this—for her, more than for him. Sienna deserved better than another Quinn screwing with her life.

"You're welcome. Adam...what's wrong?" Concern glistened in her eyes and he hated that he wanted to ease it. So he didn't.

"Nothing's wrong. Just a long day."

She reached across the table for his hand and he pulled back, instead lifting his wineglass. He saw the flash of hurt in her eyes and told himself not to acknowledge it. Pain was transitory. She'd get over this.

They both would.

Dinner had been long and quiet, Sienna thought a couple hours later. She'd sensed Adam pulling away from her even as he sat within touching distance. It was as if the man she'd known for so long had vanished into an icy shell.

And it had only gotten worse once they got home. *Home.* When had she started thinking of Adam's house as *home*? When had she begun to think that there was more between her and Adam than either of them had counted on?

When did she start to love him?

Sienna stopped on the stairs and clutched the banister. Kevin and Nick were long gone, and Adam had disappeared into his office the moment they returned. She was alone when this new, staggering realization hit her and Sienna was grateful for it.

Four years ago, when Devon Quinn rushed her through a romance, seduction and marriage, she'd convinced herself that she was in love. Now, what she felt for Adam just *eclipsed* what those feelings for Devon had been. It was like comparing a doughnut to a seven-course meal. Or a tent to a mansion.

Not only was there *more* love. There were more layers. More definition. More colors in a rainbow that she'd once thought was complete.

She sat down abruptly and looked through the black iron railing to the floor below and the hall that led to Adam's office. She remembered the sudden coolness that had sprung up between them over dinner. He'd looked at her and she could see that he was simply being polite. The heat she was accustomed to from him was banked behind a wall of distance.

Was this why? Had he guessed how she felt? Had he somehow sensed it? Was that the reason he'd changed toward her so suddenly? Oh God, she hadn't meant to love Adam. Now though, as with her house and the car, it was too late to change anything.

And she wasn't entirely sure she would change it even if she could. Love, when it finally arrived, was too big, too overwhelming, to put aside. Adam might not want it, but Sienna was going to relish these new feelings, even if it meant living with pain later.

"But for right now," she murmured as she pushed to her feet again, "he's going to talk to me. I'm not going to spend the next week or so with this cold silence surrounding me."

Wow, she sounded brave. If only she *felt* that way, too.

She wore a dark green T-shirt, denim shorts and she was barefoot, so when she took the stairs, she didn't make a sound. Sienna walked along the hall just as quietly, then tapped gently on his office door. Opening it, she peered inside. "Adam?"

The office was dark but for the brass desk lamp that sent out a small puddle of golden light. It wasn't enough to eradicate the shadows entirely, but it did manage to paint a soft spotlight on the man sitting at the edge of that glow.

Adam was lounging in one of the two burgundy leather club chairs opposite his desk, with his long legs kicked out in front of him. He had a drink in his hand, and though he looked relaxed, Sienna could nearly *feel* the tension emanating from him coming toward her in waves.

Turning his head, he looked at her and she saw that his eyes were still shuttered. "What is it?"

Hardly a warm welcome, but she'd take it. She walked to him and stopped right in front of him.

"Exactly my question. I want to know what's going on. What's happened?"

And please don't know I love you.

He took a sip from the heavy crystal tumbler he held. Then he pushed to his feet, set the glass down with a hard *click* on the desktop and swiveled back around to face her. "Nothing's happened, Sienna. It's just that playtime's over."

She swayed a little. Playtime. "What do you mean?"

He sighed, and leaned against the desk. Feet crossed at the ankles, arms folded across his chest, he couldn't have been more silently defensive.

"I mean, I'm leaving for Santa Barbara tomorrow."

Sienna frowned. "I thought your meeting was next week."

"I'm going early," he said, each word clipped.

"Why?" She had to hear him say it, though she was pretty sure she already knew the answer.

"Because this thing between us has to end, Sienna." His gaze fixed on hers, but there was no warmth in that steady brown gaze. "We both knew going in that it wouldn't last. Well, now that Delores will be taking care of the baby, we're done."

Her heart ached as if someone were squeezing it. Her stomach roiled and ice seemed to flood her veins. "Because you say so."

"That's right."

In spite of the chill she felt, Sienna faced him

squarely. "You know what, Adam? That's fine. It's over. Because *I* say so."

"Whatever helps," he muttered.

Her best intentions went right out the window. She didn't want him to know she loved him? At the moment, she couldn't have explained to herself why she *did* love him.

"Don't do that," she snapped, and stepped closer. "You don't get to brush off my feelings or act as though nothing between us has mattered—"

"Sienna…"

"—because it *has* and you know it." Her breath came fast and furious from her lungs. She was a little light-headed and starting to think she might be hyperventilating. Just what she needed, to keel over in a dead faint.

"Why does it have to mean anything beyond what it was?" he asked, his voice lazy, as if nothing mattered to him. That, more than anything else, infuriated her.

"My God, the arrogance," she said on a harsh breath.

He pushed off the desk and stood, legs braced, as if ready for a fight. Well he'd come to the right place.

"Stop it, Sienna."

"No. Not because you tell me to. Not because I promised myself I wouldn't say *I love you*."

He winced and shook his head and the ice in his eyes went deeper, colder, going from simply winter to an arctic frost. Pain opened up inside her and tears stung the backs of her eyes, but she blinked frantically, determined not to let him see them.

"Oh, you didn't want to hear that, did you?"

"No, because what would be the point?"

"Feelings are their own point, Adam." She took a breath and blew it out in exasperation. "I knew that would be your response, so I wasn't going to say it. Wasn't going to let you know how I felt because I didn't want to put you on the spot or set myself up for your dismissal." She whirled around, stalked off three paces, then spun right back again. "But you know what? The *hell* with that. Why should I keep *my* feelings to myself for *your* sake? It's clear you don't give a flying damn what I'm feeling or thinking. You've already decided that this is over.

"Well news flash, Adam. You don't decide how people feel. Or what they say or do."

Sienna couldn't remember ever being this furious. This sad. This tortured.

"I never said—"

She laughed and it sounded strained even to her. "There it is again, telling me what you didn't say instead of actually saying what you really mean. Or feel." Sienna looked him up and down and avoided meeting that cold, hard gaze again. "Your problem is that you *do* care for me. You just don't want to."

His mouth tightened until a muscle in his jaw twitched with the force of him grinding his teeth. "Damn it, Sienna, do we have to do this? Aren't you the one who said we could be friends when this was over?"

Having her own words tossed back at her was an extra slap. My God, had she really said that? Believed it?

"I was wrong. I'm not your friend. Apparently, I'm no longer your lover, either." She took a deep breath, swallowed hard and said, "But I am the woman who loves you—in spite of you being the most arrogant jackass on the face of the planet, I love you.

"I'm going to try to stop though, so spare me your pity." She turned and headed for the door. When she got there, she paused and looked back at him. "If you really think running to Santa Barbara is going to make this easier, I wish you luck with that, but you're going to be massively disappointed."

"I'm not running," he ground out.

"Keep telling yourself that." Grabbing the doorknob, she pulled it closed behind her. "Have a nice trip."

For the next two days, it was just Sienna and Jack. She didn't call Cheryl, didn't even check in at the shop beyond telling her assistant, Terri, to postpone the two appointments she had for another week or so. She was in no mood to try to be creative. To try to find the sunshine in life and capture it digitally.

How could she, when it felt as though the earth had opened up beneath her feet? Yes, she'd known going in that there would be no future with Adam. But she'd at least had the *present*. Now she had nothing.

"Just you, sweet baby," she murmured, smoothing her hand over Jack's baby-fine hair. "You, I won't give up. I can't."

She'd already lost Adam, how could she lose Jack, too? She would just have to be careful. Come to the house when she was sure Adam was at work or something. Sienna was pretty sure Delores wouldn't rat her out to Adam.

"Adam. God, I miss him," she whispered, and heard her own voice echo in the great room. Just being here now, walking through this lovely house, she saw Adam everywhere. And his absence was like a gaping hole in her heart.

She'd spent the last two nights on the sofa in the baby's room, lying awake because if she tried to sleep, Adam came to her in dreams. Cowardly maybe, to use a sleeping baby as an emotional teddy bear. But she didn't want to be alone. And couldn't bear the thought of being in Adam's room without him.

"Was it really only a little more than a week ago that this all started?" she wondered aloud as baby Jack patted her cheeks with both hands. How could everything have changed so dramatically in such a short time? How had she not noticed that she was falling in love?

"Maybe because a part of me has always loved him. And how pitiful is that? But don't worry. I'll be okay, sweetie," she said, holding Jack close, nuzzling his neck, inhaling that clean, fresh scent that spelled baby, love. "And I'll always love you, even if I'm not here. You're going to have to be patient with your uncle Adam because he loves you, too. He's crabby sometimes, but don't hold that against him."

The baby reared back and gave her a wide, toothless grin.

"Boy, I'm really going to miss you."

Before she could get all teary again though, the doorbell rang and she walked to answer it. When she opened the door, Sienna's heart dropped.

"I knew it would be *you*." Donna Quinn sailed past Sienna into the house, then spun around to face her. "One of my sons wasn't enough for you? Now you're making a play for the other one, as well?"

Ten

"I won't have it."

Donna Quinn was practically trembling with fury. Her brown eyes snapped with the force of her rage. "I won't have you here. In this house. In my son's life." She stabbed one finger at Sienna. "An old friend of mine saw you out to dinner with Adam. She called and delighted in telling me that Devon's ex was moving up the food chain in the Quinn family."

Just when Sienna had thought she'd hit rock bottom, it seemed there was further to fall.

Oh God. Adam's mother had never liked her. Never thought Sienna was the "right" woman for Devon. According to Donna, the divorce was Sienna's doing, and when Devon died, the woman had blamed Sienna for that, too. It hadn't mattered to her at the time, because Sienna never had to deal with Donna.

Looked like those days were over.

Sienna closed the front door and held on to Jack just a little tighter. She watched Donna stride up and down the entryway, her heels clacking noisily against the tiles. Her blond hair was styled into a layered bob and she wore cream-colored linen slacks and a sapphire-blue silk shirt. She would have looked the picture of elegance, but for the fury pumping off her.

"Whatever you're thinking," Donna accused, "worming your way into Adam's house, caring for Devon's son—" She stopped abruptly. Her gaze left Sienna's and landed on the baby as if she was just noticing him.

"Give him to me," Donna demanded.

Sienna actually took a step away. She didn't have the right, of course. Her former mother-in-law was Jack's grandmother, after all. But the baby's fingers took a tight grip on her hair and Sienna understood. This stranger with the loud voice was scaring him, so Sienna stood fast.

"He doesn't know you, Donna. You're scaring him."

The woman's head snapped back as if she'd been struck. "How dare you. He's *my* grandson."

"And he doesn't know you," Sienna said again,

keeping her voice quiet and low. "If you could calm down a little—"

"Calm down?" Donna choked out a laugh that sounded to Sienna like nails on a blackboard. "I find it ironic that the woman who is the cause of my anger is actually telling me to calm down."

Sienna took a breath and reminded herself to be polite. The cool quiet of the house had been shattered. Donna stood in a slash of sunlight that reflected in her eyes and almost looked like flames. In a flash, she remembered everything Adam had told her about his mother. About the way she'd hovered over Devon and pretty much ignored Adam. Sienna remembered Devon ducking his mother's phone calls. Moving to Italy to get out from under her thumb.

And yet, none of that mattered because Donna was here now, and like it or not, she was Jack's grandmother. Adam's mother. So Sienna kept a tight leash on the anger beginning to build in the pit of her stomach and reached for patience.

Then she watched as Donna swept her gaze up and down Sienna, taking in the jeans shorts, the bare feet and the gray T-shirt with a sneer. "How can I calm down when I find *you* back in our lives? My God, you're like a specter haunting the Quinn family. Wasn't it enough that Devon died because of you?"

Sienna gasped. She'd known all along that Devon's mother blamed her for his death, and she'd let it go. Because Donna wasn't a part of her life anymore and everyone needed someone to blame when tragedy struck.

But damned if she'd stand still for it now. "We were divorced for a year and a half when he died, Donna. How was it my fault?"

"Because if you had *stayed* with him," she cried, the glimmer of angry tears shining in her eyes, "he wouldn't have been on that damn boat. Or in that *stupid* race."

"God, Donna, you knew him better than that," Sienna said, trying to reach past the woman's grief. "Of course Devon would have been in the race. He always did exactly what he wanted, when he wanted. He took every chance he could because he thought he was immortal."

"You don't have the right to speak to me about *my* son."

"I have every right," Sienna said quietly, smoothing her hand up and down the baby's back in an effort to comfort him. "I was his wife."

"You never should have been. If he'd listened to me…"

Sienna sighed and Donna reacted.

"Your plan is to be Adam's wife now, isn't it?"

"No," she said, and the single word cost her because the truth was, if he had asked her to marry him she would have said yes in a blink. But he hadn't. Never would. So how she felt didn't matter.

"You'd better not even consider it," Donna said,

and swiped one hand across her cheeks to angrily wipe away a stray tear or two. Then she narrowed her gaze on Sienna. "Because Adam will never tie himself to you."

No, he wouldn't. Not because of anything his mother might do, but because Adam had decided to cut her out of his life. And it tore at Sienna to admit that to herself. She looked at Donna and tried to look past the woman's anger. Whatever she was, she had loved her son and Sienna couldn't even imagine the pain of losing him. Whether she qualified for mother of the year or not really didn't come into it.

"There's nothing between Adam and me," Sienna finally said, though it cost her. Donna didn't look convinced.

"And there won't be. I'll see to it."

Sienna could have laughed at that. No one made Adam Quinn do anything he didn't want to do. And he didn't take orders from anyone, either. Especially his mother. No reason to point that out though, since no matter what she wanted to believe, Donna knew all of this as well as Sienna did.

"Now," Donna said, her voice low and throbbing with banked emotion, "I want to hold my grandson and I would like you to leave this house."

Pure reflex had Sienna tightening her hold on the baby. "Adam's expecting me to be here, taking care of Jack."

"I'm here now. Your assistance is unnecessary." Donna reached out and scooped Jack up.

Instantly, the baby wailed and leaned toward Sienna, holding out both arms to her. Sienna's heart physically ached as she looked from the baby to the hard eyes of his grandmother. She really didn't have a choice. This wasn't her home. That wasn't her child. And Adam wasn't hers, either. The hardest truth to face.

"All right, Donna, I'll leave." Deliberately, she avoided looking at the baby, still crying for her. "Jack's food and bottles are in the kitchen pantry."

"I'll find them," Donna assured her.

"Okay, then. I'll pack and go." The other woman watched in silence as Sienna turned and walked up the stairs. Jack's heartbroken wails followed her, and Sienna's gaze blurred with tears. She held tight to the railing as she took the stairs with the slow deliberation of someone climbing the steps to the gallows.

She felt as if she'd been hollowed out and could only think that *this* was how it felt to lose everything that mattered.

Three days in Santa Barbara and it was all over but for the celebrating.

The golf course was a done deal and work on the project would start in the next couple of months. It was one of the best deals Adam had ever undertaken, and he realized he didn't give a good damn. He'd had to fight every minute to be able to concentrate because his mind had kept drifting back home to Sienna and the baby. Somehow, he thought in amazement, the three of them had become a *family*.

He scrubbed his hands over his face and tried to wipe away the thought that he'd thrown away something most people never found. But what other choice had he had? None. His track record with relationships sucked. Adam didn't want to give Sienna more pain. If she was hurt now, then that was better than more pain later on. He'd done the right thing.

So why did he feel so crappy?

Adam paced the length of the luxurious living room in the Presidential Suite. He and Kevin were in the best hotel in the city in a room that would have had Sienna sighing in pleasure—and no doubt taking pictures from every angle—and he couldn't have cared less. The place could have been a flooded-out cave for all he noticed. Or cared.

"Man," Kevin said, dropping into a chair, "we cleared this up in record time. Once we get the papers signed tonight, we can head home."

"Yeah. Thanks for taking care of that last meeting."

"I've never seen you in such a rush to get things settled and signed."

"No point in waiting around, is there?" Adam opened the French doors onto the stone balcony and leaned both hands on the wrought iron railing. It wasn't that he was in a hurry. More like he couldn't focus for the first time in his life. He leaned into the wind and hoped to hell it would blow his mind clear. But chances of that were slim.

It had been three days and he'd been reliving that last scene with Sienna ever since he left the house. He could see her face clearly, how she'd struggled to bank down tears of fury and frustration. He heard her say *I love you*. He saw her walk out of his office and close the door quietly behind her.

Didn't matter that she was hundreds of miles away. She was with him, no matter where the hell he was. He couldn't get her out of his mind. And wasn't sure he ever would. Hell, Adam figured he'd probably spend the next forty years with her image front and center in his thoughts. Torturing him. Showing him what he could have had. "Maybe that's just what I deserve."

"What's that?" Kevin called.

"Nothing," Adam told him. "Wasn't talking to you."

"Well, talking to yourself is a bad sign, son."

Adam frowned as his best friend walked out onto the balcony to join him. He was carrying two beers and handed one to Adam. "So, want to tell me why you raced through this deal like the hounds of hell were after you?"

"I didn't. Hell, you did most of the work."

"And don't think I won't remind you of that come bonus time," Kevin said cheerfully. "But I think there's more to it than that. I think you're in a hurry to get home. Hmm. Wonder why."

Adam snorted. "You couldn't be more wrong." Though a part of him wanted nothing more than to hop on his private jet and get the hell back to *her*, he knew it wouldn't do any good. When he went home, Sienna would leave. Even if Delores wasn't back from vacation yet, Sienna wouldn't stay in that house with him. Not after everything they'd said to each other. Not after they'd ended so brutally what had started out so well.

"Okay, that's a lie," Kevin said amiably.

Adam gave him a hard look.

"The patented Quinn glare never worked on me, so save it," Kevin said. "We both know you're in a hurry to get back to Sienna, but you're lying about it to me and yourself. Why?"

Adam sighed. Having a best friend who knew you so well could be a real pain in the ass sometimes. Yes, Adam wanted to get back home, and also, no, he didn't. Because once he was back home... "Let it go, Kevin."

"Not a chance." Kevin took a sip of his beer, stared out at the sea for a minute or two, then looked at Adam. "So. What did you do?"

Adam stared at him. "What makes you think I did anything?"

"Because I know you, Adam." Kevin shook his head in disgust, took another sip of his beer and leaned back against the railing. The ocean wind whipped past them both. The sun dipped behind a bank of gray clouds and below them on the sea, surfers shouted joyfully to each other as they rode waves to shore.

"Nobody likes a know-it-all, Kevin."

"Sure they do." Looking straight at him, Kevin narrowed his eyes and said, "Let's see how close I get. You told Sienna to get lost because you're sacrificing yourself to save her."

He was close but damned if Adam would admit it. He snorted. "I don't do sacrifice."

"Bull. You spent most of your whole damn life jumping onto a sacrificial altar."

"I'm not that altruistic."

"Bull again." Kevin scowled at him. "Family is what counts to you, Adam. And Devon was family."

"What's that supposed to mean?"

The sun was just beginning to set and Kevin was backlit against it. Adam had to squint to see his friend's expression and when he finally made it out, he wasn't surprised to see aggravation there.

"You took the heat with your mother to try to keep her off Devon's ass."

"Didn't work. Thanks for the reminder." Adam lifted his beer in salute and took a drink.

"You pulled all the weight with your dad to cover up the fact that Devon was a screwup."

"Nobody could please our dad," Adam countered,

thinking back to just how many times he himself had taken the blame for some mishap on a construction site because their father went easier on him than he did Devon.

"Right. Okay, still defending him." Kevin pushed off the railing and stood there, with the wind whipping through his hair. "You forget. I saw a lot of this crap, Adam, so you can't fool me."

Good point. "Fine. Whatever. I tried to help my brother. Shoot me."

"You're doing a good enough job on your own," Kevin snapped. "I've seen you and Sienna together. The two of you *work*. And you know it. Hell, there's so many sappy butterflies flying around you both I expect cartoon hearts to appear in the air over your heads."

"I could say the same about you and Nick," Adam pointed out, taking another sip of his beer, though it didn't even taste good anymore.

"Yeah, you could. The difference is, I found who I wanted and I went out and got him. You're going to let Sienna dance out of your life. Why? Because of Devon again? Just how much do you have to give up because of your no-good brother?"

"Just hold on a minute…"

"No. Screw this, Adam." Kevin set his beer down on a nearby table and crossed his arms over his chest. "Devon was selfish and lazy and didn't deserve half of the loyalty you always gave him."

Adam stiffened in automatic defense mode. Hell,

he'd been standing up for Devon their whole lives. Apparently, even death couldn't stop the knee-jerk reaction to save Devon's reputation. "He was still my brother."

"Too bad he never seemed to remember that," Kevin said grimly.

"Damn it, Kevin, he's dead. Isn't that enough?"

"Apparently not, since you're still jumping in front of bullets for him." Shaking his head, Kevin stared him down and Adam listened. "Devon never had the brains to know a good thing when he had it."

Adam raked one hand through his hair and wished he could argue with him.

Kevin's chin jutted out as if asking Adam to plant his fist on it. But they both knew that wouldn't happen. "Devon threw away his partnership in the firm you two started together."

"Yeah—"

"He turned his back on his parents, practically cutting them out of his life completely because it was easier than dealing with the family crap we *all* deal with."

"True, but he—"

"And finally," Kevin said hotly, "he let Sienna go so he could chase other women. And *these* are just some of the reasons why you've always been a better man than Devon."

"Damn it, Kevin." As much as he hated to admit it, everything his friend said was true. Hell, Kevin was more a brother to Adam than Devon ever had been and though it hurt to admit it, it was a relief to acknowledge it at last, too. Kevin had always been the one Adam could count on. Even if it was to say all the things Adam really didn't want to hear.

Grabbing up his beer, Kevin clinked his bottle to Adam's and took a drink. "So you're a better man than your idiot brother."

"Thanks. But according to you, that's a low bar."

"Now we have to find out if you're smarter than he was, too."

Adam knew exactly what he meant and said, "Hasn't she had enough of the Quinn family messing with her life?"

"Adam," Kevin asked on a sigh, "does Sienna seem like the type of woman who's going to let *any* guy run her life for her?"

He thought about that for a minute, then smiled. "No, she's really not. You were right about us redoing her house. She was so furious…"

"Yet she didn't leave you," he pointed out. "You left her."

"For her sake," Adam muttered. "I failed at marriage once before."

"Takes two, man," Kevin told him. "Believe me, I *know.* Tricia didn't hold up her end, either. Neither one of you cared enough to fight for it."

Nodding, Adam silently agreed, remembering that he and his ex-wife hadn't even really had a fight. They weren't invested enough to care, so they'd eventually just drifted apart. Now, Sienna, on the other hand—he actually enjoyed going head-to-head with her. Arguing was fun, but making up was amazing.

"You're smiling."

"Stop looking at me," Adam said, and took another sip of his beer.

"I'd rather be looking at Nick," Kevin allowed. "So? What's the plan? We get back home and you straighten this mess out while you still can?"

"If I don't, are you going to bug me about it forever?"

"I think we both know the answer to that," Kevin said, smiling.

"Yeah, we do." Adam nodded at his friend. His brother. "Let's get the paperwork wrapped up and go home."

"I'll drink to that." Kevin lifted his beer and Adam tapped his own bottle against it.

One more day and he'd fix this. Fix it all. He'd marry Sienna, they could both adopt Jack and they'd have a damn family that would make everyone who knew them jealous.

And if she argued with him about his decision? Bonus.

Adam walked into chaos.

Jack was screaming, Donna was crying and the

great room looked like a bomb had gone off in the center of it. Where the hell was Sienna?

"Mother?"

Her head snapped up and her wild gaze fixed on him. "Oh, thank God. He won't stop crying." She waved both hands at the baby. "Do something for him. It's driving me insane. There's no one to help. I'm at my wit's end…"

Adam dropped his bag, walked to the baby and lifted him out of the walker. His skin was hot and flushed; tears tracked down his cheeks and into the rings of fat around his little neck. His hair was plastered to his head and the minute Adam picked him up, Jack laid his head down on Adam's shoulder and snuffled loudly.

"What the hell is going on here?" he asked, turning his head to look around the room. "Where's Sienna?"

Donna gasped. "I sent her away. As you should have."

"You did what?" His voice went too loud and Jack cringed against him. "Sorry, sorry," he murmured, patting the boy's back while he fired a hard look at his mother.

"She didn't belong here. In your *house*. Caring for Devon's *son*. *My* grandson."

"She was invited to be here, Mother," Adam pointed out. "You weren't."

She gasped again and color rushed into her cheeks.

Adam sighed. It wouldn't do any good to fight with his mother. Better to just placate her and get rid of her.

"If you think you can take up with that woman, you're wrong."

Adam went still. "Excuse me?"

Jack's toys were strewn across the floor. There were four empty coffee cups on different tables and a few bottles of water. Cookie crumbs littered the floor under the walker and a box of diapers was sitting on the wet bar. His place was a wreck, the baby was hysterical and his mother was ready for war. Perfect.

"If you allow that woman back into our family, I'll never speak to you again."

Drama. His whole damn life had been drama.

Donna Quinn knew how to create a scene better than any Hollywood director. She was known for being able to bloodlessly flail someone alive until they were nothing more than a hank of hair and a bag of bones. But Adam hadn't played her game since he was a kid, so he wasn't quite sure why she thought this would work on him now.

"Mother," he said evenly, "you don't run my life. Never have. I make my own choices and I'll see any woman I want to. I don't need your permission."

"She's *evil*," Donna insisted. "She as good as killed your brother because she didn't care enough to stay with him. Take care of him."

"Oh for God's sake." He hitched Jack higher on his shoulder when he realized the baby had fallen asleep. "Devon cheated on her regularly and didn't bother to hide it. Sienna would have been crazy to stay with him."

"You don't understand. You never did," Donna said as tears welled up and spilled down her cheeks. "You were always more your father's than mine."

"I don't know, Mother," he said, tiredly. He'd come home to face Sienna. To find a way to make a future. To convince her to take a chance on yet another Quinn. Instead, he was thrown into a B movie starring a woman who seemed determined to cling to the drama he wanted to avoid. "Maybe that's true. What I *do* know, is that I'm going to see Sienna. And I'm going to bring her home. Here. If you can't handle that, I suggest you go back to Florida."

"You're throwing your own mother out?"

"No," he corrected, looking into her teary eyes. A part of him felt sorry for her. She'd been a ghost in his life, never really putting in the time, but he didn't doubt that she had loved him and Devon. In her own way. But Adam's priority was Sienna now. Sienna and Jack. If his mother couldn't accept that…

"I'm asking you to stop blaming everyone but Devon for what happened," he said quietly.

"If I can't?"

"Then I'll be sorry about it. But, you can take my jet back home. I'll call the airport and tell them to get it ready for you."

She stared at him, horrified for a moment or two. "You've chosen her over me."

"I've chosen the future over the past," he corrected and the moment the words left him, they felt right.

"Then I'm leaving."

"That's your choice," he said, wishing things were different—as he had most of his life. "I'll call the airport."

Donna stared at him for a long moment as if she couldn't quite believe how this scene had gone. In her mind, he was sure, she'd imagined Adam apologizing to her and promising to turn Sienna out of his life forever. Well, she'd have to learn to live with disappointment.

Donna sniffed heroically, then hurried from the room, one hand to her mouth as if holding back more tears. She would go back to Florida and whether she came back to visit or not would be up to her. But it was time she realized as he had, that Adam was done with what Kevin had called *jumping onto the sacrificial altar*.

"Okay, kiddo," he whispered, kissing the baby, who lay sound asleep against his chest. "Time to go find our woman."

Sienna hunched over her computer, studying the photos she'd taken the day before at the beach. Since leaving Adam's house, she'd tried to focus. To reclaim her own life and lose herself in her job.

So far, it wasn't working, but she had high hopes. She hadn't cried all day today, so that was a plus. She still wasn't sleeping though and spent the nights curled up on her couch watching dreadful old movies, just for the company.

But every day it was bound to get a little better, right? Because the way she was feeling, there was just nowhere to go but up.

When the doorbell rang, she went to answer it and caught a glimpse of a shiny black Jaguar parked at her curb. Her heart leaped in her chest and she had to swallow hard past a knot of longing that lodged in her throat. She knew it was Adam. It had to be— because she simply didn't know anyone else who owned a car like that one.

Why was he here? What could he want? Hope lifted in the center of her chest and she batted it back down. She couldn't stand to pump up her balloon again only to have it popped.

Steeling herself, she opened the door and simply stared. His hair was shaggy and windblown. He wore a dark red T-shirt, blue jeans and a worn pair of brown cowboy boots. She was so used to seeing him either naked or in elegantly tailored suits, she had to take a second to appreciate the casual Adam.

He held Jack in his arms and as she looked at him, the baby squealed and threw himself at her. Sienna grabbed him and snuggled him close, reveling in the warm, solid weight of him. Then she looked up into Adam's eyes and her heartbeat stuttered. There were no shutters in those brown depths. He wasn't trying to keep her out anymore and she didn't know what to make of that.

Jack squirmed excitedly and she laughed as she wrapped both arms around him. "Oh, I've missed you so much," she whispered, and planted a kiss on his forehead.

"Did you miss me, too?" Adam asked, walking into the house, forcing her to back up so he could come in and close the door behind him.

She'd missed him as she would have her arm. Her leg. Her heart. "Adam…"

"Just answer the question, Sienna."

"Of course I missed you," she snapped, irritated that the moment they were together, he started issuing orders again.

He grinned. "You don't sound happy about that."

"Why would I be? I tell you I love you and you basically say 'go away'?" She blew out a breath. "Not exactly hearts and flowers, Adam."

"Yeah," he said, frowning, "about that. That's why I'm here." He took a deep breath and said, "I was wrong."

Sienna blinked at him.

"Surprise." He scrubbed the back of his neck and for the first time, Sienna realized Mr. King of the Universe looked nervous.

"Yes," he continued, "I can admit when I'm

wrong. It doesn't happen often because I'm usually right."

"Of course you are." Sienna laughed helplessly. "So what were you wrong about exactly?"

He walked past her into the tiny living room and began to pace it like a tiger in a too-small cage. "Nice room. Tiny, though."

"Thank you," she said wryly.

He glared at her. "You know, I already failed at marriage once."

"Yes, we've been over that," she reminded him. "I have, too."

"Yeah, but that's different. Devon was an ass. Wasn't your fault. Me? I'm no good at sharing." He shot her a look and Sienna saw the flash of worry in his eyes. This was the first time she could ever remember seeing Adam less than supremely confident.

"Adam—"

"Oh, and I'm sorry for any hideous thing my mother said to you."

She flushed and leaned her forehead against the baby's. "Not necessary. I understand."

"Well I don't." Adam scowled again, came to a stop and crossed his arms over his chest. "I want you to know, I don't care what my mother—or anyone else for that matter—thinks. I don't care that I sucked at marriage before, either, because being married to *you* would be different."

"Married?" Her heartbeat jumped into a gallop.

Was he proposing? If so, it was a terrible one and she wished he'd be quiet long enough for her to say yes.

"You love me, Sienna. Even if you hadn't told me, I'd have known. It's written all over your face." He walked right up to her, tipped her chin up and stared down into her eyes. "I see it whenever I look at you. And I don't think I can go another day without seeing it again."

She took a breath and said, "Oh, Adam, I—"

"No point in you saying no, because this is just the way it has to be." He gave her a hard look. "You love me. I love you. We get married. Delores can help us out with Jack when we need it—you know, if we both have to work and neither of us can take him with us…"

"I'm sure she could, but—"

Adam stared at the ceiling for a second, thinking, then said, "Of course, when we have more kids, Delores will need help—"

"More kids?"

He shrugged. "Big house. You don't want Jack growing up alone, do you?"

"No, but we should—"

"Maybe we could get Delores's sister to move here. We could build a casita in the backyard, big enough for both of them and—"

"Casita?"

"You know, small house—mother-in-law quarters—" He broke off. "Don't worry though, not for your mother-in-law."

Her head was spinning, her heart was racing and breathing was really becoming an issue. "Adam, what exactly are you trying to say?"

"I'm trying to tell you you're going to marry me," he said.

Jack squealed, reached for Adam. He took the tiny boy into his arms so easily it was as if he'd been born handling a baby. Funny how quickly things could change, Sienna thought. Yesterday her heart had been broken. Today, Adam was here, offering her love. A family.

"I'm going to marry you?"

"Damn straight you are." With his free arm, Adam pulled her up close. "I love you, Sienna. I tried not to. I thought about staying away from you. To protect you. But I can't. If that makes me a selfish bastard, I'll have to live with it.

"I can't let you go. Don't want to live without you and I'm not sure I could. I want us—the three of us—to live in that big empty house. I want us to have more kids, too. Jack needs some brothers and sisters and we're getting pretty good at the kid thing, so why not?"

"Why not?" she repeated, nodding, crying, blinking her eyes because she didn't want to miss a moment of this.

"I think we should adopt Jack right away," he went

on, and ran the palm of his hand over the back of the baby's head. "Be officially his parents, you know?"

She laid one hand on Adam's chest and felt his heart racing as quickly as hers. "I think that's a wonderful idea."

"Good. That's good." He kissed her, lingering over her mouth as if he were savoring the most delectable taste in the world. When he finally lifted his head again, he said, "We'll have to find a way to deal with my mother. But I promise you, she won't ever interfere with what's between us."

"I know that, Adam," Sienna said, reaching up to cup his cheek in the palm of her hand. Donna Quinn was an unhappy woman, but maybe someday, Sienna thought, there would be peace between them all.

He bent for another kiss and the baby slapped them both, laughing gleefully. "Okay," Adam said with a grin, "I think he approves. So. You still haven't said. Are you going to marry me or not?"

Sienna laughed. God, she felt wonderful. "Wow. A question. Sure you don't want to just order me to marry you?"

"It would be easier," he admitted. "But yeah. A question. That needs an answer."

"Then here it is. Absolutely yes, Adam." Sienna smiled up at the man who had held her heart almost from the moment she'd first met him. It had taken time for them to find each other. But the waiting had only made this beginning that much sweeter.

She wrapped her arms around Adam and laid her head on his chest alongside the boy who was already the son of her heart. The three of them completed a circle that Sienna hadn't even known she'd been searching for. And now that she'd found it, she knew she was home.

"So," Adam whispered. "To go ring shopping, we'll have to leave Hermione here and take Thor."

She tipped her head back to look at him, a smile curving her mouth. "Hermione?"

Adam shrugged. "You're not the only one who can name a car."

"But Hermione?" Sienna was grinning now, so happy she felt like she just might explode with it.

"It's British and I liked those Harry Potter books."

Laughing, Sienna said, "I really love you."

Adam kissed her hard. "Don't ever stop."

Epilogue

One year later...

"Lift Jack a little higher," Sienna ordered. "And move Maya more to the left. No my left. Your right."

"Sienna," Adam grumbled, "this shot is for us, not the Sistine Chapel. Can you just take the picture?"

"Just a minute," Nick said, and darted in front of the camera to straighten Maya's tiny, pale green dress. "There you go, my little goddaughter. You look beautiful." He turned to Jack to tickle the little boy's ribs, gaining a giggle for his trouble. "And that handsome boy." He slipped out of the way again. "Okay, Sienna, get it fast!"

She did, the click of her camera sounding like a

whole herd of crickets set loose in the photography studio. When she was satisfied, she straightened up, walked to her family and scooped the two-month-old girl into her arms. "There we go, sweet baby girl."

Adam swung Jack up to his shoulders as he stood up and looked over at Nick. "Where's Kevin?"

"He took the boys into the backyard." Nick grinned. "All three of them get a little antsy when they're forced to sit still for pictures."

Sienna listened to everyone and smiled. The last year had been the most perfect one of her life. Married to Adam, mother to Jack and then, like a blessing, a mother again to baby Maya.

The world was pretty much a beautiful place and she thanked Whoever was listening every night for the wonder of her life.

"Hey," Adam said, coming in close to claim a kiss from her and to drop one on his daughter's forehead. "You okay?"

She looked up into brown eyes that were never closed to her these days. Sienna read warmth and happiness in his steady gaze and her heart simply filled up and spilled over into her soul.

"I'm excellent," she assured him.

"Good, I settle for nothing less than the best." Adam dropped one arm around her shoulders and hooked his other arm across Jack's feet, holding him in place.

"I'll get Kevin and the boys, then we can head

to our place for dinner." Nick grinned and headed down the hallway toward the backyard. No doubt, the boys were on the swing set or drawing at one of the tables. Sienna kept several items in the yard to use as props for kids' pictures, and to occupy children who hated being cooped up inside.

Sienna watched him go and leaned into Adam with a satisfied smile. "Who knew that Kevin would be so into being a daddy?"

"I think Nick always knew," Adam said, dropping a kiss on the top of her head. "Those kids already have Kevin wrapped around their fingers."

Two brothers—Max, three and Tony, five—had joined Kevin and Nick's family as foster children six months before. And already they were talking adoption. Nick had never been happier and Kevin carried so many photos of the boys around to show off, people at the office were actively avoiding him now.

Adam's mother hadn't exactly turned into Mary Poppins, but she had made an effort in the last few months. The woman was crazy about her grandchildren—in small doses—so Sienna had hope that one day, old wounds would heal over.

Meanwhile, Sienna had her perfect photography studio and she'd sold her little house in Long Beach to a lovely young couple who promised to take good care of it. Her business was growing by leaps and bounds, and every day, she got to go home to the people she loved most in the world.

"What're you thinking?" Adam whispered.

"About how much I love you. And the kids. And our life."

"Our life together is everything to me. I don't know how I lived before you, Sienna," he said softly, and his eyes showed her the love that colored those words.

"I love you, Adam," she said, stroking her fingertips along his cheek.

"And when we get these kids to bed later," he said with a wink, "I'll show you how much I love you."

"More mistakes?" she teased, reminding him of how they started.

Staring deeply into her eyes, Adam said, "Best mistake I ever made. It brought me to you."

* * * * *

If you liked this **BILLIONAIRES AND BABIES**
novel from Maureen Child,
don't miss her other books in this series!

BABY BONANZA
DOUBLE THE TROUBLE
TRIPLE THE FUN
THE BABY INHERITANCE

Or her **PREGNANT BY THE BOSS** *trilogy!*

HAVING HER BOSS'S BABY
A BABY FOR THE BOSS
SNOWBOUND WITH THE BOSS

Available now from Harlequin Desire!

***

And don't miss the next
BILLIONAIRES AND BABIES *story*
THE BABY GAME *by Rhonda Russell*
Available July 2018!

***

If you're on Twitter, tell us what you think of
Harlequin Desire! #harlequindesire

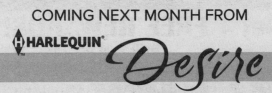

Get 4 FREE REWARDS!

We'll send you 2 FREE Books plus 2 FREE Mystery Gifts.

Harlequin® Desire books feature heroes who have it all: wealth, status, incredible good looks... everything but the right woman.

FREE Value Over $20

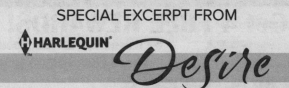
Cody McNeill knew—instantly—that the lovely redhead
seated in the booth across the way had mistaken him for
his twin.

His whole life, he'd witnessed women stare at Carson in
just that manner—like he was the answer to all their fantasies.
It was strange, really, since he and Carson were supposedly
identical. To people who knew them, they couldn't be more
different. Even strangers could usually tell at a glance that
Carson was the charmer and Cody was...not.

But somehow the redhead hadn't quite figured it out yet.

Between the dark mood hovering over Cody and the
realization that he wouldn't mind stealing away one of his
brother's admirers, he did something he hadn't done since
he was a schoolkid.

He pretended to be his twin.

"Would you like some tips on what's edible around
here?" He tested out the words with a smile.

"Edible?"

"On the menu," he clarified. "There are some good
options if you'd like input."

The way she blushed, he had to wonder what she'd thought he meant.

And damned if that intriguing notion didn't distract him from his dark mood.

"I, um…" She bit her lip uncertainly before seeming to collect her thoughts. "I'm not hungry, but thank you. I actually followed you in here to speak to you."

Ah, hell. He wasn't ready to end the game that had taken a turn for the interesting. But it was one thing to ride the wave of the woman's mistaken assumption. It was another to lie, and Cody's ethics weren't going to allow him to sink that low.

The smile his brother normally wore slid from Cody's face. Disappointment cooled the heat in his veins.

The music in the bar switched to a slow tempo that gave him an idea for putting off a conversation he didn't care to have.

"Are you sure you want to talk?" Shoving himself to his feet, he extended a hand to her. "We could dance instead."

He stared down into those green-gold eyes, willing her to say yes. But then, surprise of all surprises, the sweetest smile curved her lips, transforming her face from pretty to…

Wow.

"That sounds great," she agreed with a breathless laugh. "Thank you."

Sliding her cool fingers into his palm, she rose and let him lead her to the dance floor.

Don't miss
THE FORBIDDEN BROTHER by Joanne Rock,
part of her McNEILL MAGNATES series!

Available July 2018 wherever
Harlequin® Desire books and ebooks are sold.

www.Harlequin.com

Want to give in to temptation with steamy tales of irresistible desire?

Check out **Harlequin® Presents®**, **Harlequin® Desire** and **Harlequin® Kimani™ Romance** books!

New books available every month!